The Galactic Culinary Society

Cryovacked & Other Tales

D.R. Schoel

ISBN: 978-1-7773133-9-5

Follow D.R. Schoel on Facebook @drschoel
& Twitter @drschoel2013

Cover art by Josh Newton
https://www.instagram.com/joshnewtonart/

Layout & title design by Dakota Randall
www.dakotarandall.com

CONTENTS

THE SECRETS OF UMAMI

...While most of our members undoubtedly consider a new dish at their favorite bistro to be the zenith of their gastronomic adventures, we must all agree that galaxy-renowned Chef Hunter, Jeane Oberon, though unfortunately human, was among the top culinary researchers of our Society. In her long, illustrious career, she is recorded to have encountered failure on only one ill-fated occasion...

Excerpt from the Galactic Culinary Society's
Milky Way Review, Vol III, edition 2, N°496

-1-

Somewhere within the sweltering jungle mountains of Alpha Boötis, Jeane Oberon, in her mud-encrusted flight suit, wearily climbed up a steep slope. Suddenly, out of thick foliage, a rusting spacecraft loomed before her, scorched and shattered.

She looked up at it, her face slick with sweat. Forgetting how tired she was, she excitedly scrambled in, stepping carefully over the charred bones scattered among the creeping vines. Hunting through the ruins, she quickly found the object of her search. A blackened computer. She eagerly pried off the cover and extracted the still gleaming CPU, dropping it in her pocket.

Behind the CPU was the memory chip, and biting her lip, she ever-so-carefully pulled it out.

Then she felt something poke her in the back.

"You may turn around, female *Mudling*, but slowly!"

Jeane silently chastised herself for being careless so close to her goal. "I think you mean, *Earthling*." She surreptitiously slipped the memory chip in her pocket, raised her hands, and turned around.

"Enlighten me. Who in their right mind would name themselves after the... the *dirt* of their homeworld?"

Jeane was familiar with the Greelons: one of the four major planet-nations. It raised a tentacle, aiming its disintegrator pistol at her, and burbled from behind its water-mask, "Now, *Dirtling*, the memory chip!"

Jeane towered over the creature which came up to her waist, half her six foot three. She considered her options. A quick punch to the faceplate containing the liquid methane of its native ocean? No. It looked too intent on using its disintegrator. Stall for time, then.

"I'm not sure what you're talking about. I'm just... sight-seeing."

"Oh, puh-lease. You think I don't recognize you? You're a celebrity. You're here for your precious *Society*, are you not? An underling at the Greelon Bureau of Records tipped me off that you'd been snooping around and were interested in Captain Hoargar's lost trade ship."

"Seems like it wasn't so lost-"

"Those were sealed records, by the way!"

Jeane shrugged. "And what brings you?"

"As you well know: the legendary *Edible Sonnets of Umami*! If there's something to be found after all these years, it's something *my business* can profit from! Now, I can't risk disintegrating you and the memory chip, so if I just reduce this, to disintegrate your head..."

The business-alien fiddled uncertainly with a knob on his pistol. He didn't look familiar with the weapon. He might do something accidentally, Jeane thought.

"Alright." She slowly lowered her hands, searched in her pocket, and drew out a computer chip. The Greelon's eyestalks followed the silver chip in the palm of her hand with satisfaction. She extended it to him.

"Oops." She dropped the chip and her boot was poised over it before the Greelon knew what had happened.

"Throw your gun down, or else-"

"Or else, what?" The Greelon narrowed his eyestalks at her, calling her bluff. "You wouldn't dare."

"Try me?"

"I don't believe you." The Greelon slithered back, aiming its pistol.

Jeane lowered her boot. There was a soft crunch. The Greelon's eyes nearly popped out of its eyestalks in disbelief. She removed her boot, revealing the crushed, useless computer chip.

She casually sauntered past the dumbstruck alien, "I told you."

"Wait!" The Greelon slithered up and put a soft, moist tentacle on her shoulder. "I must congratulate you," it sneered, tapping her on the back, "for having the ink-sacks to destroy the most potent secret in the universe!"

-2-

Jeane patiently stood on the floor of the dimly lit amphitheatre. Three aliens were seated above her and behind them the lecture hall was packed to capacity with a hundred different species, all members of the Galactic Culinary Society, in an uproar of hooting and hollering.

"Order, order! Let her speak." The Ansul Overseer, Achiro Mifune, pounded his gavel.

Achiro had an ancient, sloth-like face. Long, silver-haired limbs poked out of his purple robes. The Triumvirate was represented by three of the major races: the Ansul, Moaperdarians, and the Skylar (Greelons generally looked down on the Society and its charitable goals).

"What she says can't be true!" a Gefiltafysh called from the back of the hall. "Kick out the human!" another inconspicuous voice shouted.

Achiro pounded his gavel. The Moaperdarian Overseer, Ol' Sands, turned to the crowd, "Now, now, behave yourselves! Further outbursts will lead to ejection and possible dismemberment." Ol' Sands spoke in an authoritative voice, cutting through the din. Her beady eyes were clouded and blind, set into a mole-like face.

"She means we'll lose our membership if we keep it up, or… be torn limb from limb…?" someone at the back of the hall whispered nervously.

Ol' Sands continued, "Please recall the purpose of these gatherings. By collecting and cataloguing the dining habits and rites of the countless peoples of the galaxy, and *sharing* these findings, we bring all sentients closer together. We impart universal goodwill. Remember our motto: to Preserve and Serve!"

Various calls of *Hear! Hear!*

"Agreed. Let us listen to what the *Earthman* has to say," the third Overseer, Lord Hawktalon of the Skylar, impatiently declared.

Jeane held her tongue. No point correcting him. The Skylar were famously condescending, believing themselves to be the preeminent race in the universe. His face was hidden by a featureless white mask, as per the custom of his kind.

Lord Hawktalon folded his hands disdainfully, "*Now…* Let us hear your absurd claim."

Jeane held up the memory chip she had recovered. She'd fooled the Greelon, stepping on the outmoded CPU — which she'd taken out of her pocket instead of the memory chip — but the alien hadn't been able to tell the difference.

"I've recovered Captain Hoargar's logbook. And his final entry."

A hush fell on the hall. The three Overseers leaned forward.

"What have you learned?"

"Hoargar was a trader on his way to Alpha Boötis when he decided to stop at *Umami*, along his route."

"The Edible Sonnets of Umami were known throughout the galaxy in those days. But in our times, they're almost forgotten." Achiro sadly shrugged hairy shoulders.

Murmurs ran through the amphitheatre. Much of the membership, naturally (being interested in culinary arcana), had heard tales of Hoargar and the legendary Sonnets, though others, from faraway quadrants, had not. Still, even among those who knew the name, *Umami*, there were conflicting reports. Whispered questioning filled the air.

Jeane went on, "*The monks of Umami* opened their doors to Hoargar. They welcomed all visitors and even accepted some who expressed an interest to study their ways-"

"But, but, hold on - What *are* the Edible Sonnets of Umami?!" the frustrated Gefiltafysh called out, on behalf of much of the hall.

"According to legend," Ol' Sands answered, "*digestible poetry*."

"Words you could *eat*?" someone else blurted incredulously.

Jeane concurred, "The last report is from over a century ago. Those who stayed with the monks uniformly explained it that way, though their recollections are all vague and confused. What's most intriguing is that every being described the same experience. Everyone who's *listened* -if that's the right word- to the Sonnets, has claimed it's the most incredible thing in the universe they've... *tasted*."

"And we all know how subjective taste is," Lord Hawktalon snorted.

"So, they were drugged!" someone called out.

"Skeptics tested themselves. No abnormal substances were ever found," Ol' Sands replied. "It's a mystery."

Mutterings of disbelief coursed through the benches.

Jeane waited for the voices to die down. "Before continuing this debate, why not let Captain Hoargar speak for himself?"

She pressed a button and a transparent *hologlobe* lowered from the ceiling. Within, a flickering image came to life. The hall fell into attentive silence.

-3-

Captain Hoargar had his back to the recording camera; his leafy green skin and yellow mustachios were visible behind an upturned collar. Before him, half-a-dozen Greelons in black uniforms floated. Still more swarmed in through the overhead airlock.

Hoargar had clandestinely turned on the recording when the Greelons boarded. Through a narrow viewport, a large Greelon War Cruiser could be seen, grappling hooks wrapped around Hoargar's vessel.

A Greelon in a chrome and brass water-mask and golden epaulettes was berating the captain, while the rest trained plasma bayonets on him. "So, you thought you could hinder us by turning off the gravity, eh? Not my crack troops, Hoargar!"

"Oh, no, no. I routinely turn it off. Have you seen the price of graviton particles these days?" Hoargar answered civilly, though his gruffness was unmistakable.

The Greelon sneered, "The galactic rumor mill has been working overtime. A trusted informant has informed us, through a second trusted informant who heard from a third... ahem, it suffices to state we've heard you're in possession of valuable information... from the monks of Umami!"

"Hardly reason to stop my ship. What use can it be to you?" Hoargar growled.

"What use, you ask?" the Greelon Commander threw his tentacles up in mock wonderment. "What use? You are undoubtedly aware, having recently visited there, that those hapless monks bestow upon pilgrims their universally loved Sonnets... for F–R–E-E!"

"So, it's profiteering, is it?"

"Imagine the unimaginable riches! Though I suspect, from what we've heard of the *infamous* Captain Hoargar, you already have."

Even while the Greelon Commander spoke, his troops flung themselves from one bulkhead to the next, tentacles pulling and grabbing with expert deftness in the zero-gravity, natives of an ocean world after all, while they attached small, silver, blinking orbs throughout the compartment.

Those in the hall of the Galactic Culinary Society watched with growing concern, but there was nothing they could do. These events had already come to their grim conclusion, two hundred years before.

"It's fortunate for me then that I was escorted out of the monks' cloisters... er, I mean, I voluntarily left, empty-handed."

"Is that so? Perhaps you'd like to add a trifle to your tale, no? Perhaps, I can convince you." The

Commander clapped two tentacles. The blinking orbs which the soldiers had attached to the bulkheads began flashing red. In unison, they started a dire countdown: "Ten, nine..."

Hoargar hesitated stoically for a moment, then blurted, "Alright! I smuggled out a fruit-"

"A fruit!" the Commander laughed.

"...eight, seven..."

"Yes, a fruit that's vital to-"

But the Commander was having none of it. "An important... *fruit*, you say? Don't pull my tentacles!"

Meantime, his troops glanced about nervously. "Uhm, Commander?"

"...six, five..."

Hoargar was speechless. There was nothing more he could add.

"Very well! Have it your way, Captain!"

The Greelons beat a hasty retreat, pushing and shoving to get out the airlock.

"Four, three..."

Through the viewport, the War Cruiser could be seen releasing its grapples and blasting away, leaving the serene, green disk of Alpha Boötis in its wake.

"...two..."

Captain Hoargar stared at the stars, his shoulders slumped in resignation.

"...one."

Everything turned to white.

-4-

"So," Lord Hawktalon concluded as the image faded, "he found nothing! And you've gathered us - for nothing!"

"Not quite." Jeane raised her finger. "Hoargar mentioned he stole a fruit, a *Dragon Fruit*, to be precise. It's in the logbook. From a quick reading of the monks' scrolls, he must have realized it was a key element in the Sonnets' preparation."

"And yet," Achiro woefully shook his shaggy mane, "there are no more Dragon Fruit on Umami. Their world is now practically barren."

"I know. But according to Hoargar's records, on his way from Umami to Alpha Boötis he took a significant detour. There can only be one reason. I believe he planted his Dragon Fruit, which grew in a specific climate, in similar environmental conditions that he found on *Arcturus*, before being stopped by the Greelons."

"Need I remind you," Ol' Sands quietly broke in, "that there are also no more monks of Umami. Their people have abandoned their dying planet."

"I've heard there's one monk left. That's why I'm here, to ask for the Society's assistance to finance an expedition to Arcturus—"

Lord Hawktalon cut her off. "An expedition? How much will that cost? You Earthmen are indeed brazen, based on what you've shown us!"

"And what about my request for a utensils museum?" a bloated Dobeian shouted.

Jeane drove on doggedly. "Listen to me, if I bring the last monk a Dragon Fruit, since there's no more on his homeworld, and there's no reason he should believe any more exist *anywhere*, then he might agree to teach me. That's why I need to go to Arcturus, to get the Dragon Fruit. Shouldn't we preserve and protect the ancient ways of Umami?"

Silence fell over the hall as her words sunk in. A chance to uncover and learn the secrets of the Edible Sonnets! Jeane looked at each of the Overseers in turn. What were they thinking? Would they help?

At last Ol' Sands spoke, "You depend on many suppositions, Jeane Oberon. *If* Hoargar planted his Dragon Fruit on Arcturus as you surmise, did it flower and thrive? I'm sorry to say, it's unlikely. And even if this so-called last monk exists, does he truly know how to recreate the Sonnets? Let us suppose he does. While I may admire you and your work, what makes you so confident this monk will agree to teach *you*?

"Therefore, considering the uncertain nature of your project and our limited resources," she turned warily to the Dobeian who'd requested a utensils museum, "the Society will move forward with your proposal only if there's unanimous agreement among the Triumvirate."

The air tingled with suspense. Hands, digits, claws, and feelers gripped their seat benches.

"What say you?" Ol' Sands turned to Achiro, sitting pensively to her left.

The Ansul pointed a hairy finger at Jeane, "You've not failed us before Jeane Oberon, so I will trust you now."

He turned to Ol' Sands, awaiting her response. The Moaperdarian, though blind, seemed to look deeply into Jeane. "To my mind this expedition is a long shot, and so I am inclined to vote nay," murmurs ran through the hall, "*however*, however, even if we were to refuse you, I'm certain you'd find a way to pursue the Sonnets, is that not so?"

Jeane nodded.

"So, I see no reason why the Society should not participate in the risks if we also wish to share in the glory. I will agree."

Applause broke out.

Lord Hawktalon raised his hand, "I have not spoken. I have not spoken!" He leaned forward menacingly. "This whole project is hopeless. I vote, no!"

Angry shouts. Lord Hawktalon grabbed the gavel from Achiro, pounding it on the table. "I have not finished! I'd be willing to change my vote, if," from behind his featureless mask he was certainly narrowing his eyes at Jeane (if he had eyes), "the Earthman consents to reimburse the Society, if he fails!"

Without hesitation Jeane answered, "I agree."

"You are overconfident, Earthman. I very much doubt you have the funds. Will you sign over your ship as collateral?"

Jeane clenched her jaw. "Understood."

"Very well. Beyond the usually expensive clearances through the Astrogates, fuel costs, and blah, blah, what else do you require?"

"Sensor equipment designed according to my specifications - to locate the Dragon Fruit, rappelling gear, and a heat suit capable of withstanding 2,000 degrees."

-5-

Soon, Jeane was hurtling from the Society's Headquarters through the Astrolink: an ageless, interstellar structure of sentient-made wormholes. Shortly after, her single-seat craft was parked near the rim of a volcano on Arcturus, twenty-two kilometers high, nearly as tall as Olympus Mons on Mars.

Ominous clouds gathered at the summit.

Hooking her rappelling anchor into blackened pumice, she donned a breathing mask. The hydrogen sulfide fumes weren't too bad up here, but it would get a lot worse at the bottom. The descent would take the better part of two days.

Peering down, she saw a long dark funnel simmering with a hellish glow. Roiling at the bottom: a blood-red lava lake. She could feel its heat even at this great height.

Jeane locked the belaying rope to the karabiner on her harness and quickly lowered herself over the lip, occasionally taking small hops, controlling her speed with the break-end of the rope in her left hand.

In the upper part of the cone, the encircling walls looked like they'd been splattered with massive gobs of tar, undulating in overlapping waves and smears. Hardened lava.

After a day's toil, she'd descended halfway into the throat of the beast, judiciously laying out her lines.

She made camp on a thin ledge, drinking water out of a straw inserted in her mask. Careful not to dehydrate. It was a hundred-and-four-degrees Fahrenheit.

Laying her head back to rest for the first time since starting out, she glanced at the rock wall entombing her. The stone was a kaleidoscope of colors, fused by the intense heat of ancient eruptions. Orange, blue, iridescent yellows; like going to sleep in a jewel box. Hard to image Hoargar making this same trip into the bowels of the volcano two hundred years before to plant the Dragon Fruit.

If it was down there, and she was convinced it was, he'd apparently hoped to return for it someday. Unless, Jeane wondered, fatigued, what if she really was on a wild goose chase? Had she pushed herself too hard this time?

It didn't matter. She'd opened a Pandora's box by digging up Captain Hoargar's logbook.

She had to uncover the true nature of the Sonnets before anyone else.

-6-

Jeane's preset alarm woke her after four hours. She put on her aluminized heat suit, necessary for the final leg.

She shot down in one smooth rappel, working the stiffness out of her joints. Looking up, the opening of the volcano was a tiny oval, revealing dark, mustard colored clouds.

She descended in long bounds, down, down, down.

Her wrist computer flashed: *One Thousand Degrees.*

Below her feet the lava lake bubbled and frothed, like an angry milkshake about to explode.

Fourteen Hundred Degrees.

The air was distorted with heat, but the rock nearby looked different. She scrabbled edgewise to get a better view.

"GCS Journal Report: The rock is porous here. I've found methanogenic lichen. It appears to live off carbon dioxide and heat. The lichen's burrowed deeply. During an eruption, the outer layers probably get burned off, but I guess it grows back to capture energy. Still no sign of the Dragon

Fruit."

Near her hand, a pearlescent hydrothermal worm wriggled through the black methanogenic moss, tunneling its way into the stone.

"I'm continuing my descent."

The rumbling and roaring intensified. Jeane turned off her external audio and set her vision shade to maximum.

Nineteen hundred degrees.

The rock around her shook vigorously, like she was clinging to a massive wall of jelly. The lava field boiled in all directions, a hundred meters below.

Two thousand degrees. Suit maximum temperature.

Where was the damn thing?

A yellowish rain began to patter down, steaming as it fell.

Two thousand and ten.

"I think I've found something."

Through a haze of heat and sweat, Jeane saw a strange, small shape, round and smooth. Tendril-like roots grew into the rock.

Yellow rain hissed as it came into contact with her suit. Hydrochloric acid. She ignored it, reached down, and plucked the Dragon Fruit.

Glancing along the interior rim of the volcano, she saw dozens more just below her feet. She edged lengthwise, looking for a foothold to get closer.

Then her rappel lines came tumbling down. Dissolved by the acid rain.

Shoving the Dragon Fruit in her pouch, she glanced up, grim-faced and saw a small, anti-gravity powered, rhodium plated dronebot descend through the smoke and fumes, its exquisite, silver-hued hull reflecting lava flames. It appeared to be specifically designed for its task, something Jeane (and the cash-strapped Society) never could have afforded.

It serenely lowered itself past her and extended a thin, robotic arm, plucking a dozen Dragon Fruit.

Mission accomplished, it floated upwards, past Jeane.

"Hey, I can use some help here."

The dronebot continued its upward trajectory, rudely ignoring her.

"Hey, you!"

The silvery speck disappeared over the rim of the volcano.

"Hey!"

No response. Jeane gritted her teeth.

She began the long climb up.

By hand.

-7-

Four days later, she landed on Umami.

Boundless tundra — greenish, gray moss — struggled among endless miles of barren rock and boulder.

Shouldering her pack, Jeane turned to the mountains and walked thoughtfully (and a little sorely) up a path where stout, yellow dwarf shrubs did their best imitations of real plants on this dry, chilly planet. She couldn't guess how long it would take to convince the monk to take her in, but she planned to stay for as long as necessary.

After a half-day's walk up the twisting path, she looked ahead and saw it, the monastery, perched on a cliff edge.

Crumbling, white-washed towers with partially collapsed, gabled wooden roofs were piled one atop another, hugging a sheer mountain wall.

The place was in a pitiable state of disrepair. It looked abandoned.

Jeane knocked on a rusting, metal door, thinking how to present her case—*if* there was anyone home. Her knocking echoed in the valley.

Suddenly, the door opened, creaking on worn-out hinges.

Two green points, like eyes, peered out.

"Hello," Jeane said cheerfully.

A strange alien floated in the shadows.

"Mmm, welcome and good day. Do come in, dearest. We've been expecting you," it croaked.

Jeane paused, taken aback.

"Come, come."

On her guard, she followed the creature inside.

In the gloomy light, filtered through broken windows, she recognized it as a Dobeian. Native of Dobe, a gas-giant planet. A soft-bodied, balloon-shaped thing filled with helium. Pulsating its gas-bag body, it pushed itself through the air, trailing half-a-dozen tendrils or thin, manipulative appendages.

"You have brought one for me as well, mmm?" The Dobeian glanced back at her. It wore vision goggles which glinted greenly, like computer screens.

"You knew I was coming?" Jeane asked.

"There's one here who precedes you. But if you please, my name is Brother Otin."

Otin floated into an open courtyard, or sky-well, surrounded by desolate buildings where Jeane saw the Greelon warming its tentacles by a fire-pit in the middle of the yard.

"Hullo, Soiling! I was beginning to wonder when you'd get here!" An open sack with a dozen Dragon Fruit lay by its side.

"So, it was your dronebot that left me on

Arcturus."

"*Pft.* I knew you'd be ok. You're resourceful. Another story for your Society, huh?"

Jeane sat on the opposite bench. He'd beaten her to the punch.

"Don't look so glum! I suppose you're wondering how I did it? Indeed, it's thanks to you! You thought you could outwit me, hmmm? Greelons are not so easily fooled, and certainly not I, *Xstersiisterpeeze.* I knew you were up to something when you stepped on that microchip, so I slapped a micro-tracker on your shoulder."

Jeane reached for her back.

"Oh, don't worry, it's dissolved by now. The manufacturer claims there shouldn't be any allergic reactions, but you never know." It shrugged its tentacles.

"Go on."

"The rest was easy. I spied on the Society's gathering and followed you to Arcturus with, I may add, a rather expensive and well crafted dronebot, built with a hundred percent made in Greelon parts. Designed by our top Ansul in-residence engineer, naturally. Greelon craftsmanship, granted, can be a bit shoddy *at times*, so I hire only the best designers from Ansul. Fortunately, they're more interested in making *things*, than... salary." It rubbed its tentacles together greedily.

Brother Otin hovered near, "I shall prepare your room." It floated off with Jeane's pack. She kept the

Dragon Fruit with her in her pouch.

As soon as the Dobeian was out of earshot, Xstersiisterpeeze leaned forward and whispered conspiratorially, "I'm not sure the good monk has all his," the Greelon twirled a tentacle, pointing behind his eyestalks, "three brains in order. He's yet to acknowledge my offer. I've requested to become an acolyte, as per your plan, in exchange for the strange vegetable."

"It's a fruit. It flowers."

"Indeed? I don't care. Between me and you, of course." It held up one of the Dragon Fruit from its bag. A lustrous purple when first picked, it cooled to a dull pink, like a cat's tongue. "It's so very soft to the touch. Yet equally firm. Sour smelling. Actually, I've given Brother Otin one already, free of charge." He looked slantwise at Jeane, as if he possessed a secret he couldn't help divulging, "And last night, he prepared an Edible Sonnet for me!"

Jeane listened.

"Ah... What was it like, you ask? Flavorful sparks exploded in my mind like fireworks! As if each point on my tongue had invited my brains to a heavenly party! And what about the words? Did they have meaning? It seemed nonsense. But I wonder? It would be like... like asking if flavor can have meaning, or words can have flavor? Is it possible? Blissful sensation! I *must* have the recipe!" The Greelon smiled stupidly through its water-mask, emitting little bubbles.

"It is true." Brother Otin floated into the

courtyard. "I've been painstakingly considering his proposition. To *experience* the Sonnets is for all. That is their purpose! But to learn to create?" The Dobeian turned toward Jeane. "May I presume you too, like Xstersi... ister... err... whatever his name is, equally desire to learn the Art of the Esculent Sonnets?" It raised a delicate tendril expectantly.

Jeane reached into her pouch and took out the Dragon Fruit, which Brother Otin accepted.

"Very well then. Each of you wish to learn the Secret? As you can surely see, I am not a native of Umami, but traveled here, like you, to be initiated into the Mysteries. And I believe your presence is a sign our Order is meant to live on; its light won't be extinguished! However, I had to supplicate myself for many months, fasting and meditating, before the Last Monk, may the Ancestral Spirits consecrate his bones, decided to teach me, but we can dispense with all that."

The impatient Greelon breathed a sigh of relief.

"However," Otin raised a tendril, "the Old Monk insisted the Mysteries were so deep, so intense, so intricate... so *mysterious*, he could only possibly teach one student at a time." His words hung in the air. "Which of you two should I choose?"

Jeane glared daggers at Xstersiisterpeeze.

He glared nuclear warheads at her.

The Dobeian floated to Jeane, "may I please examine your tongue?"

Jeane complied with the strange request. Brother Otin peered closely, like a doctor conducting an examination, his goggle lenses flashing.

"And now, Xister-si… Xstersiister… Xstersisiii-"

"Don't trouble yourself, Brother Otin. Don't you recall, you examined me when I arrived?"

Otin shrugged his tendrils as if to say there was no helping it. The Greelon sighed and pressed a button on his facemask. The liquid in it burbled into a small tank on his back. The glass covering popped open and holding his breath, the Greelon stuck out his grey tongue.

"Hmm… very good, very good."

With a gasp, Xstersiisterpeeze closed his breathing mask.

Otin declared, "You are both tongue pure! Thusly, you are both eligible for the Order. So, how to solve this dilemma?"

Brother Otin was silent for a few minutes. Finally, he slapped a tendril on his gaseous hide. "I have it! I will agree to teach whoever wins at… four contests! Is that not agreeable? The getting of the Dragon Fruit was the first test."

"Good, then I'm winning," the Greelon said.

Brother Otin waved a dismissive tendril. "You were unawares to begin, so we'll call it a tie."

"That's not fair! I got more."

"Tut-tut," Brother Otin was warming to his idea. "We shall begin tomorrow. But firstly, I must express my gratitude to you for these," he pointed a lightly trembling tendril at the Greelon's bag, "and for the one you brought too, my dear. Each one is precious. Without Dragon Fruit, it's been a sad time since the passing of my Master, and each year seems to get colder. Since Xstersissy... uh... *he*, has already experienced what all pilgrims journey here for, it is only proper I invite you, tall one, to join me tonight in the Grand Stupa for a tasting, or should I say 'reading', of the Esculent Sonnets of Umami!"

-8-

Faint starlight sparkled through the broken rafters of the domed ceiling.

Brother Otin placidly floated behind a wooden table in the midst of the chamber. Jeane stood before him.

On the table, she saw five small ink pots in a row. Next to these was a thin, partially transparent square sheet, like rice paper.

Brother Otin picked up five brushes, one in each of his tendrils.

Indefinable smells stirred in the air.

'A feather swallows
the Great Ocean-'

Jeane watched as a brush was dipped in a pot. She saw its tip emerge lava-red, reminding her of the Dragon Fruit. With a swift stroke, Otin drew the first line of the poem. A spectral light from his visors reflected on the white sheet.

'Polishing bricks to
make a mirror-'

Another brush dipped. Black. An ideogram depicting the second line transposed over the first. Jeane tasted a hint of bitterness on the wind, blowing through the rafters.

> *'The waterfall below*
> *the Thoughtless*
> *Cliff-'*

Dip. A swirl of golden yellow. Sweetness.

> *'But when P'An*
> *ku dispersed the*
> *nebula-'*

White. The taste of salt in the air, like an ocean breeze.

> *'The impure parted*
> *from the pure.'*

A final stroke of marine blue, with a heart-warming, savory aroma.

Brother Otin put aside his brushes. With expert deftness, his tendrils folded the translucent sheet with colored markings until it was no larger than a wafer.

He floated toward Jeane, "directly on your tongue please, while it's still fresh in your mind."

Jeane held out her tongue. Otin gently placed it

there, like a lozenge. He smiled beneficently and floated back to his writing table, sighing deeply, indeed pleasurably, at the completion of his task.

Jeane had to admit, it was the greatest thing she'd ever tasted.

-9-

In the morning, under the bright though hardly warming sun of Umami, Brother Otin led Jeane and Xstersiisterpeeze down a rambling mountain path for the first (or actually second) test.

Trailing behind the Dobeian, Xstersiisterpeeze asked Jeane, "Well, Soiling, how did you find it? What'd you think of the Sonnets?"

"I suppose I had the same experience as you."

"Mm-hmm. Any clue how it was accomplished?"

"No idea… so far."

"Waddaya think the gas-bag has planned for us?"

"We'll see."

Otin stopped in front of a large stone pile. The rocks had been arranged into a mound about seven feet high.

"The Tomb of Our Ancestors, may the Spirits consecrate their bones!" Otin announced, raising his tendrils to the sky, stopping a good ten feet from the cairn.

They heard an angry buzzing in the air.

"The Long-Haired Honeybee Test!" Otin nodded toward the mound. He was carrying a short scoop and a wooden bowl. "So, who wants to go first?"

Jeane saw thousands of bees swarming around and about the tall pile of neatly placed rock; they'd turned it into their hive.

"In these ever-cooling conditions, there isn't much left for the Long-Haired Bee to pollinate, though fortunately the sturdy Cloud Berry bush remains. We monks have been practicing apiculture for millennia."

A large bee hovered near Jeane and Xstersiisterpeeze, buzzing furiously in their ears. They saw it had long hairs, or setae, in orange and black stripes circling its fat body, which was twice as large as Jeane's thumb.

"So, uhm, you smoke 'em out?" Xstersiisterpeeze asked hopefully.

"We prefer not to disturb the bees," Otin replied.

"Protective gear then?"

Otin shook his head.

Xstersiisterpeeze eyed the buzzing hive dubiously, "Ah, in that case, Soilings first if you please." He waved his tentacle toward the cairn.

Jeane took the scoop and bowl from Otin. She calmly approached.

Hundreds of bees swarmed around her irritably in a black cloud, but she continued forward in unhurried, measured steps.

"Oh, it's too terrible to bear! It's not worth it!" The Greelon winced.

Nearing the cairn, Jeane examined its surface, noticing a rock at about waist height, protruding as though previously removed.

She grasped it firmly, but it was stuck.

"Come back, Earthling! Give it up before it's too late! Ah, I can't watch!" The Greelon covered his eyestalks with his tentacles.

Coolly passing her hand over the stone to brush away some hairy bees, Jeane noticed it was sealed with a brownish glue: *propolis*, a resin-like mixture produced by the insects.

Picking a small, sharp-edged stone off the ground, she cut the propolis. She pulled out the stone very slowly so as not to upset the bees.

With the hive uncapped, she slid her scoop in, splitting a wax-sealed honeycomb. She drew out a spoonful of golden honey.

Without altering her even pace, Jeane returned.

"Ahhh. It's a test to overcome one's fear!" Xstersiisterpeeze slapped his tentacles together, as it dawned on him.

"Maybe," Jeane whispered, "but the bees on Umami have no stinger."

Xstersiisterpeeze's eyestalks widened in surprise, "you mean the ol' monk's been playing us?"

Fearless now, the Greelon swiftly picked up the scoop and bowl. He hurried into the swarm, waving bees away with multiple appendages.

Squeezing in a long, flexible tentacle lined with suction cups, he sucked out twice as much honey as Jeane.

He returned triumphantly with gloopy honey

dripping all over, "Har! You Dirtlings are so gullible! And *you* thought I was *afraid?!*"

-10-

"The third test: The Savory Blue Fish Sauce Contest!"

This time, Brother Otin had led them to a rock-strewn beach. A wide river faced them.

Xstersiisterpeeze looked around uncertainly. "What are we supposed to do here?"

"It appears we're to produce the fish for the fish sauce," Jeane surmised.

"What a lovely, lovely day. I do so enjoy the air!" The monk floated along, pulling a cart. "Now, it's time for my afternoon hymnals and the lighting of the oil lamps, so I shall return to the monastery. I trust you'll play fair?"

Xstersiisterpeeze glanced in the cart. There were two barrels. They were both empty. Except for this, there was nothing else for miles around other than scattered rocks and boulders, not even a lonely tree.

"What are we supposed to catch the fish with?" the Greelon called after Brother Otin, who was already floating away.

Otin turned around, "Oh, I nearly forgot. You are

not to leave the beach. Not until you've completed your task."

Xstersiisterpeeze pointed up the mountain path they'd come down, where there was a patch of desolate shrubbery. "Can we go there?"

"Do not touch the Cloud Berry bush if you please. You may make use of whatever else is available on the beach."

"But there's nothing on the beach?!"

Brother Otin floated off, ignoring the Greelon's pleas, "Good luck!"

"It looks like you have an advantage over me again," Jeane said.

"How do you mean?"

"You're a cephalopod."

Xstersiisterpeeze snorted, "Oh, please. I haven't chased anything since I was a hatchling. We're not primitives, you know."

"But on your homeworld, you live underwater."

"Yes. In great and magnificent cities. I dine at only the finest establishments. My dinner is *brought* to me. Is it otherwise on your dusty little planet? Do you still go sneaking through the jungle with... whatever you hunted with? Sharpened sticks?"

Jeane nodded. "You've got it."

Grumbling, Xstersiisterpeeze approached the shoreline. "Maybe I ought to give it a go," he mumbled to himself. "It might come back to me."

Meanwhile, Jeane looked around. Rocks. The cart. Two barrels.

"He said we could use anything on the beach…"

She took one of the barrels from the cart and carried it to the water. She waded in up to her waist.

Schools of small, silvery-blue fish-creatures darted just beneath the surface like flashing shadows. She swept the barrel through the water, using it as a net.

Up on the beach, Xstersiisterpeeze watched. "I think she's on to something." He grabbed the remaining barrel and sploshed in.

But Jeane wasn't having any success. The fish simply skipped out of the way. Eventually, she might catch one or two if she remained perfectly still, but there had to be a better method…

She glanced at the shore again. *All those rocks…*

She sloshed back to the beach and put the barrel down. She began carrying rocks into the shallows, building up two walls into a trench which reached the surface of the water. While she worked, Xstersiisterpeeze zipped this way and that with his barrel without success.

After an hour's labor, she judged the trench was long enough. She retrieved her barrel, capping one end with it. But how to get the fish in the trench and then into the barrel, and then take them out? She'd require at least ten arms.

"Hey, Xster!"

He bobbed his head up.

"Any luck?"

"Not so far, Dirtling. But, if I–"

"I think we're going to have to do this together."

Noticing the trench she'd built, Xstersiisterpeeze swam closer, "Hmm, very clever. I see. Herd the fish down this narrowing lane you've constructed, and directly into the barrel."

"Yes, but it needs one person to hold the barrel, and another to drive the fish in. You'll make a good fish-herder."

Xstersiisterpeeze looked at her suspiciously, "Indeed! You hold the barrel then make off with all the fish!"

"We have two barrels. Let's say, the first one is mine–or yours, whichever you prefer. So long as we agree in advance. We do it twice. Whoever has the most fish in their barrel…"

Xstersiisterpeeze eyed her uncertainly, debating her proposal over in his mind.

"Unfortunately, we don't have any other choice but to trust each other."

At last, a scheming light entered the Greelon's eyes, "Alright! It's a deal." He popped open his water-mask, spat on a tentacle and shook with Jeane. "I'll go first! That barrel you're holding is mine, agreed?"

Jeane nodded and crouched over the barrel at one end of the trench.

Xstersiisterpeeze swam around to the other, lying perfectly still until he saw a school of blue fish swim unsuspectingly into position.

The Greelon suddenly shot out with all tentacles splayed and swirling. He drove the fish into the trench. They sped into the barrel, which Jeane quickly turned upright before they could get out.

"Hah, hah! We did it!" the Greelon shouted. "You single-brained Dirtlings are not as stupid as you look!"

Together, they dragged the barrel onto the beach, drained it (careful not to let the fish out) and put it on the cart.

Jeane then carried the second barrel into the river, positioning it at the end of the trench.

"Xstersiisterpeeze?"

She looked up to see the Greelon hurrying away with the cart behind him.

He huffed and puffed. "Remember, you agreed. This one's mine! What's the old saying: fool you once, shame on *you*, fool you twice... I'm a genius! Hah, hah! The Sonnets will be mine!"

He left her high and dry.

-11-

A pink sunset bathed the monastery perched on the mountainside in a fiery glow.

Strolling the abandoned hallways, Jeane found Otin at the bottom of crumbling stone steps leading to an open-air atrium.

Three stone vessels, four feet in diameter, were set into the tiled floor and capped with wooden covers. Otin opened one of these, dumping in the fish the Greelon had brought back earlier.

"I'm not disturbing you, am I?"

"Certainly not, my dear."

"You don't mind if I tour the premises?"

"If you can't sleep, you can always lend a tendril." Brother Otin extended a long, broom-sized ladle.

Jeane took it and stirred the fish.

"Don't be afraid to pound them. Break them up. That's it. My, you humans are strong."

"Why do I get the feeling *all* we've been doing here is simply your ordinary work?"

"Hmm. It's always good to have helping tendrils." Otin uncapped the second casket. Jeane saw it was filled with a slurry of mashed fish fermenting in their own liquid. The monk scooped some into a large ceramic jug, before pouring it through a strainer into the third vessel.

Leaning over as she stirred, Jeane observed it came out clear, blue, and gleaming. A savory aroma filled the air, reminding her of the Sonnets.

"Keep stirring! Keep stirring! That's it!" Brother Otin floated down a narrow lane, disappearing round the bend. His voice drifted back as he mused to himself, "My, my, having acolytes is so very useful."

Jeane paused in her stirring. Where'd he gone to? She quietly put down the ladle and padded to the bend.

To one side of the adjoining courtyard was an old, grease-covered machine with rollers and a press. Baskets brimming with small, chocolate colored nuts were scattered about and their tiny, dried up seeds littered the floor and the machine itself which Jeane figured was used to press the nut for its oil.

At the further end of the courtyard, Jeane saw Otin hovering near an open door leading to a brick-walled chamber.

He removed his vision goggles, hanging them on a wooden peg by the door. "Too much smoke for these." Where his eyes should be were two dark orifices, like nostrils. Of course! She should have remembered Dobeian anatomy. They relied more on smell, but the orifices also collected light (however poorly), so Dobeian eyes and nose were a single organ. He obviously used his goggles to enhance his vision, but did it have another purpose?

She snuck over to the door, lifted the goggles off the peg, and passed her wrist-computer over them.

"Ah! My favorite part of the day!" Otin gurgled with pleasure from inside the chamber.

Finishing her examination, she put the goggles back. She stole a glance into the room. Wafting smoke drifted out. It smelled bitter with a hint of nuttiness, though not unpleasant.

She saw that along all four walls were racks laden with row upon row of strange black devices: small, soot covered braziers, turned upside down. An orange glow quivered under the rim of each, as though cupping tiny, golden stars. Curling black smoke drifted up from beneath.

In the center of all this, Otin held a large bowl in one tendril and a brush in another.

With yet another tendril, he lifted one of the blackened braziers, revealing a wavering flame, burning from a tin of oil.

He quickly brushed the ash which had gathered in the brazier into his bowl.

Then, using all his tendrils and picking up extra brushes, he uncapped *all* the hundreds of braziers, sweeping more and more ash into his collection bowl. He whirled and twirled, as if engaged in a frenzied, ecstatic dance, picking up speed, and spinning.

In minutes, he was done. He picked a gourd from the floor and poured a clear liquid–pure water–into the bowl, stirring until the ash blended into a fine, black ink.

Next, Otin unrolled a sheet of translucent white paper, the same as he'd used for the Sonnets, and drew a few elegant lines. He hummed, apparently satisfied with the results.

Having seen and learned enough, Jeane quietly withdrew before she was discovered.

-12-

"This is it," exclaimed Xstersiisterpeeze, "the final test!" The Greelon and Jeane stood side by side, alone in a rusting, metal-cage elevator descending, with fits and starts, into a black mine shaft.

Xstersiisterpeeze glanced sidelong at her, "Ah, I see you have that look on your face. I know you better than you know yourself, *Mudling*. You didn't come here to preserve the ancient ways of Umami from defilement! You came for one thing and one thing only: to know the truth!"

Getting no reaction out of her, Xstersiisterpeeze rolled his eyestalks. They passed a flickering light indicating their depth underground, "Brother Otin said to exit at the bottom. I hope the generators hold out."

"Don't worry, I don't think the elevator ride is part of the test," Jeane replied curtly.

"Who's worried?"

"On the other hand, there hasn't been any maintenance on these mines in over a century."

They continued in silence, watching the grey rock of the shaft pass under the lights of the elevator. Of course, Xstersiisterpeeze couldn't hold his tongue for long: "Salt mines! This time, it's who brings back the most *N-a-C-l.* I've been thinking... he must use it for the Sonnets, eh? Everything we've been gathering seems to be an ingredient."

"I've noticed the pattern."

"But how does it all come together? How do the words of the poem affect the ingredients, or vice versa?"

Jeane remained silent.

"And what was that gas-bag saying about worms? To be careful of the worm?"

With a clang, the elevator came to a sudden, jarring halt. The cage doors creaked open.

Jeane and Xstersiisterpeeze stepped out, flicking on their flashlights. Their beams played on the walls of a long, dark tunnel. They advanced cautiously.

"You know, I live under the ocean, but going this far underground still gives me the *heebee jeebees.* Why aren't there any lights?"

Jeane didn't answer but carefully examined the rock surface with her flashlight. Xstersiisterpeeze followed, "though I suppose you, being a Soiling, are in your element down here."

She ran her hand along the rough, granite-like wall. Xstersiisterpeeze imitated her, rubbing a tentacle on the rock, "I don't see any salt veins, do you? It's just plain ol' rock."

"There's more to it than that. If this is a mine tunnel made by the ancient monks of Umami, where are the supporting beams and struts?"

"Maybe, it's a natural tunnel?"

"Look how perfectly rounded the tunnel walls are. No. Something bore its way through here."

"What kind of *something*?"

The beam of Jeane's flashlight fell on an object lying on the floor, glinting. She approached to investigate.

She held up what looked like a rusting cylinder, not much bigger than her forearm. A few buttons were on it. A similar device lay nearby.

"A laser cutter," she said.

Xstersiisterpeeze picked up the second cutter, putting his fears to rest. "You see? The tunnel was made with these."

"No, they're too small to cut through all this."

"Maybe there's more abandoned equipment somewhere? The tunnel looks like it goes on forever-"

A booming howl cut him off, echoing from the dark deep, ahead.

"Oh, crap." Xstersiisterpeeze slunk behind Jeane.

The ground trembled beneath their feet. *Something* was approaching. It emitted faint sparkles, illuminating the darkness like a distant lightning storm.

"I'm, uh, just gonna observe from over here." Xstersiisterpeeze hightailed it back to the elevator. Jeane held her ground.

A giant, gleaming white worm emerged out of the shadows, its hide like ivory. It undulated, pushing its way through the earth, shaking the walls all around them; bits of rock tumbled from the ceiling. It opened its gaping maw and roared.

Jeane saw it was semi-translucent, electrical pulses flashing dimly within its body.

"Earthling! Hurry!" Xstersiisterpeeze called from the elevator.

"Hold on-"

"Hold on? For what?!"

"The worm's body appears to consist of halite."

"Halite? You mean… salt?"

Indeed, the worm was crystalline, ions pulsing through its vast length.

Xstersiisterpeeze looked down at the laser cutter he still clutched, thinking greedily of winning the contest.

"Stand aside, Soiling!"

"Just a minute, remember what Brother Otin said-"

It was too late. Xstersiisterpeeze blasted away, slicing the salt worm in two.

"Ah-hah! It's mine! You were too slow!" Xstersiisterpeeze approached the inert halves of the worm, "Boy oh boy, I've made quite a haul this time."

"I think Otin was trying to tell us to take care; he didn't mean we needed to watch out, but rather to treat the worm carefully."

Xstersiisterpeeze poked a segmented end with his laser cutter. "What're you babbling about?"

"You've heard what happens when you cut a

worm in two?"

"You mean the urban legend that you'll get two new worms? That's nonsense. Every hatchling knows it's not true."

"You're right, for common annelids. But this one looks like it belongs to the planarian genus."

"Meaning?"

"It can regenerate. Even after decapitation. And the new worms retain the memories of the old. *Both* of them. On Earth we have similar creatures, though they're practically microscopic. I think Otin left the laser cutters to gather shavings from its hide, not to…"

Even as they talked, the crystalline regeneration process had begun at a rapid-fire pace.

"Fiddlesticks," Xstersiisterpeeze said. "You can't fool me out of my winnings."

The two new salt worms reared up behind him.

"Xster-"

"Don't be a sore loser. Take solace in the fact you competed against a Greelon, so you never had a chance," *Baff! Paff!* "Gahh!"

The two worms took turns beating the Greelon.

Jeane aimed her laser cutter at the ceiling. Rock came plummeting down.

Cut off from the retreating worms by the rock-fall, Jeane grabbed the battered Greelon by a tentacle and dragged him into the elevator.

-13-

Under silver starlight, Jeane and Xstersiisterpeeze sat next to one another in the open courtyard where Brother Otin had first proposed the contest for the Edible Sonnets of Umami, warming their hands and tentacles by a crackling fire.

One of the Greelon's tentacles was in a sling and he was swathed and wrapped with bandages; he sat glumly, head hung low, with a long crack across his water-mask.

"Tsk, tsk. Didn't I tell you to be careful with poor Franky?" Otin floated over the fire, its heat sending him up like a balloon under the stars.

"I wouldn't be too hard on him, Brother Otin," Jeane said. "On the bright side, you now have *two* salt worms."

The Dobeian lazily descended. "Hmm. You perhaps have a point. Yes, I think I shall name his sibling, Herby. Yes, Franky and Herby. That's not too bad."

"Appropriate names for giant worms," Jeane agreed.

"But now, to business. I have summoned you to tally your scores."

Xstersiisterpeeze perked up, confident he had more points on the board, so to speak.

"Concerning the first test, the collection of the Dragon Fruit, as stated at the outset, you were both successful. Thusly, I have allocated a point to you each, though considering that Xstersiss... Xsterseesee... uhm... he... collected more, I have, upon reflection, decided to assign an extra half-point."

Xstersiisterpeeze stuck out his tongue at Jeane.

"Regarding the second test, the Long-Haired Honeybee test, you both extracted the honey-"

"Yeah, an' I got twice as much!" Xstersiisterpeeze interrupted. "And I wasn't afraid for a second. Not even a nanosecond."

"Yes, well, I'm sorry to inform you, it was not a test about conquering one's fears. It was meant to demonstrate your knowledge of the planet Umami. In this instance, that our bees have no protective stinger. The point goes to the human."

Xstersiisterpeeze slouched grumpily.

"On to the third test, the Blue Fish Sauce contest-"

"Surely I won that one. She didn't bring back *anything*!"

"That is true. Yet, it was not about who brought back more. It was a cooperation test. Only by working together could you get the fish. It was the human who ascertained this. So, she gets another point."

"Oh, puh-lease..."

"As for the fourth and final test, it really was about who would bring back the most salt. At this, you both failed… However, since the human risked herself *and* potentially forfeited the entire competition by choosing to save you, instead of pursuing the salt worm, it's only fair to credit her another point."

"Bah!" The Greelon threw up his tentacles in disgust.

"As you have undoubtedly noticed, each of the tests involved collecting one of the ingredients used in writing a Sonnet, but there's much more to it than that! Oh yes, there's still much more to learn."

Brother Otin paused contemplatively, looking across the smoky fire. "*However*, the Greelon has made a proposal for a very, very substantial sum, I might add, to bring the Edible Sonnets to market across the galaxy. I have considered it." The Dobeian glanced about at the ruins of the monastery. "With these riches, I would be able to restart the Order of Umami and restore it to its former glory." He fixed Jeane with his greenly lit goggles, "Franchising is but a small price to pay. So, I'm sorry to say it my dear, but *you* lose."

-14-

Jeane Oberon again stood before the Triumvirate of the Galactic Culinary Society. This time, the benches filling the hall behind them were empty.

"The prodigal Earthman has returned," Lord Hawktalon sneered derisively. He held up a glossy looking box upon which was written *Greelon Edible Sonnets*. "I'm surprised you have the temerity to show yourself, considering how it's turned out. Why have you bothered to come? You have failed, as predicted."

"I would like you to first try the Greelon Sonnets," Jeane calmly replied.

From behind his white mask, Lord Hawktalon undoubtedly scowled. At length, he passed the box across to Achiro Mifune, the Ansul Overseer.

Achiro tore it open and extracted a silver, vacuum-sealed foil package. With long, hairy fingers, he ripped the seal and took out a single, yellowish wafer with colorful markings. He carefully placed it on his tongue and munched leisurely.

"Well?" Jeane asked.

Mulling it over, Achiro finally replied, "It's

delicious."

"But is it what you expected? Does it live up to the legend of the Sonnets of Umami?"

Achiro hesitated. At length, he said, "It does not. I have tasted better."

Ol' Sands, the blind Moaperdarian, leaned forward, "Tell us Jeane, what are you getting at?"

"I first became suspicious of Brother Otin, the last monk of Umami, and his motives when it became clear the tests he put before Xstersiisterpeeze and myself were nothing more than his ordinary, everyday labors... primarily involving the collection of the ingredients for the Sonnets.

Consider this: each of the five pictograms he drew for my Sonnet consisted of one of the five *tastes* fundamental to every species, at least in our common family of sentients. These tastes represent vital molecules we crave, since our bodies can't produce them.

The ingredients used by the monks occur in their purest, distilled form. For example, the Dragon Fruit tastes *sour* because of its hydrogen ion concentration. Long ago, the monks had to dive for the Dragon Fruit where it grew near hydrothermal vents under the ocean, but with the cooling of their planet, those vents have gone out.

The Long-Haired Bee's honey is obviously sweet, satisfying our craving for carbohydrates–energy—which even bacteria need and can detect.

Shavings from the salt worm, err-*worms*-are,

it's needless to say, salty, while the oil ash mixed into an edible black ink is bitter. The fish sauce provided the fifth and final flavor, *Umami*, or *savory*, for which the monks and their homeworld are named. It provides glutamate, which acts as a neurotransmitter–in fact, the most abundant neurotransmitter found in the nervous system of all sentients. Essential for higher brain functioning." She paused, watching the Overseers for their reaction.

Ol' Sands nodded at Jeane's precise summation. "You may proceed."

"Brother Otin never intended for me to win," Jeane said. "Before my arrival, he was already contemplating how to get the highest price out of the Greelon for the secret of the Sonnets. Xstersiisterpeeze's initial offer, businessman that he is, was very stingy. So, what's the best way to raise the price? To have more than one bidder. Market demand. But, when I fortuitously showed up, Otin realized I'd never be able to outbid the Greelon, so he hit on his idea for a competition, knowing full well that if the Greelon were to lose —and the tests were designed for Xstersiisterpeeze to lose, playing against his nature, then Otin could drive up his asking price, astronomically."

"But, what about the *words*? Did you, or did you not, discover the true nature of the Edible Sonnets?" Lord Hawktalon interjected impatiently, though by now he too was engrossed in Jeane's account.

"Thank you, I was just getting to that. Before the start of the competition, Brother Otin examined my tongue with special visors, ostensibly to see if I was 'tongue pure'. This is all part of an ancient charade played by the monks of Umami. Now, bear with me; on Earth, we used to have something called the *tongue taste map*, which divides the tongue into exclusive taste sections for bitterness, sourness, saltiness, and sweetness. When it was devised, we hadn't yet discovered the fifth essential flavor, *savory*. In any event, it's long since been discredited though it now seems there was a tiny fraction of truth in it.

"Please, Lord Hawktalon, I don't know if you have eyes, but I can tell you're rolling them. If I may continue? When Otin examined my tongue, and he did the same for Xstersiisterpeeze, he was in actuality *mapping* our tongues. I had the chance to examine his goggles and copied its software to my wrist computer, but it was encrypted. It took time for the computers on my ship to crack the code.

"To sum up, our tongues were mapped with an ingenious system created by the original monks: it charts the ideal taste map according to each individual's papillae, or taste buds.

"Each verse of the Sonnet is really a unique pictogram generated by a computer algorithm. Brother Otin's goggles project these pictograms onto edible paper, which only he can see, and he then traces them, though it takes years of training and skill for a high level of precision. The words are otherwise meaningless.

"As the five flavors are applied–each in the form of a separate line of the poem–and the wafer is folded, the pictograms combine, and when placed on the tongue it perfectly aligns to each person's layout of taste receptors."

Ol' Sands was flabbergasted. "But... but, that can't be it? A robot could do it. How can a robot replicate the highest form of gustatory art? You can't be right."

Jeane shrugged. "I believe it's best if we keep the Secrets of Umami... secret. This way, the Galactic Culinary Society can preserve the truth, the Greelons get their business while the fad lasts, and Brother Otin can continue the Order of Umami with the infusion of money. Everybody wins."

"Everybody wins," Lord Hawktalon added coldly, but with a hint of reluctance now, "except you. In order to keep this secret, you will have to publicly admit failure. Furthermore, abiding by our initial agreement, you must forfeit your ship."

"I understand," Jeane said, fully aware of what she needed to do. "Now, before I take my leave, if you'd like, I can prepare an Esculent Sonnet of Umami for you each."

The three Overseers looked at her in wonder.

"I won't need the goggles–I retrieved your tongue profiles from Record Keeping—I've been doing a little practice."

She placed five flavorful ink pots before them

and unfolded three sheets of pearly white, translucent paper. "It's alright, Lord Hawktalon, you can turn around to remove your mask and carefully place the wafer yourself. I won't look."

Picking up her brush, Jeane recited, in turn, three poems, writing with swift, deft strokes.

"Quickly now, while it's fresh in your minds."

The Overseers ate.

And fell out of their chairs, in sheer bliss.

Jeane smiled, allowing, "I guess, there *might* be some art to it, after all."

-*fin*-

SONG OF THE GOLDEN BREW

Beer /bir/ *n*: **1**: an alcoholic beverage made from fermented cereal grains and brewed on any number of inhabited planets. **2**: after water and tea, the most popular drink in the universe.

The Book of Zythology
from the Galactic Culinary Society's archives

-1-

Soon, she would find out if coming all this way had been worth it, but the clock was ticking. Swimming over a lifeless coral reef, Jeane Oberon pushed on against the swiftly moving current. Far above, distant sunlight gleamed through the silvery ice crust which enveloped the entire planet of Cor Caroli.

Bone-chilling cold invaded Jeane's thermal wet suit, but she ignored it. All of her attention was focused on the gray, ancient reef which had once teemed with intelligent life.

She glanced at her chronometer. Twenty-two minutes left of air. She knew it would take ten minutes to reach the surface and another five to track back to the hole she'd cut in the ten-foot ice-crust. As a last resort she could cut another opening with the laser, but that would take time too.

Still, a few more minutes was worth the risk. All her painstaking research pointed to *this* being the spot.

Treading in place with her flippers, Jeane angled her helmet light so it shined on a piece of ashen-looking coral. Did she see? Yes, there. Embedded along one side were faint scratch marks. *Runes*, she excitedly realized. Ancient writing. And was that mark intended to refer to a type of salt? She consulted the dictionary she'd built up over two long years on her wrist computer. Yes, definitely salt. The next marking—a type of indigenous sea cucumber? And there, clear indications for the seeds of bottom growing seaweed. Jeane smiled to herself.

She'd discovered the recipe from a long extinct race for pickled sea cucumbers.

As the only human member in the *Galactic Culinary Society,* Jeane Oberon prided herself on being the best Chef Hunter, the number one field researcher, going where no one else dared to.

"They told me I'd find you down here. *Brr!* It's freezing!" Bobbing behind her was a small squid-like creature, half her six foot three, though he was most definitely not a native of Cor Caroli. "Next time you visit a water-covered planet, I recommend my homeworld, *Greelon.* It's tropical compared to this ice-cube!"

Jeane ignored the alien interloper. Maybe if she didn't say anything, he'd just... go away?

"I know you can hear me." He tapped his methane-water mask (since he couldn't breathe the liquid nitrogen which made up the ocean of Cor Caroli). "I'm on the GCS frequency."

"I'm a bit busy just now." *Nineteen minutes of air.*

"I can see that. Do you think I'm stupid? I knew you'd never answer my messages. That's why I came here personally. I need your help, Jeane."

Now, that took her by surprise. She and the alien were rivals in gourmet circles. While Jeane pursued the tenets of the Society, *to Serve and Preserve*, the Greelon (with the unpronounceable name, *Xstersiisterpeeze*) cared only, to the best of her knowledge, about making a dishonest buck.

"Make it quick, Xstersi."

"Did you know that on the planet Kazaak," began the Greelon, "it's said they have an ethanolic beverage which induces mood improvement, even feelings of euphoria, and one can drink as much as one likes without *any* negative side effects?"

"That's what you came here to tell me about?" Jeane grumbled. With half her mind still on her discovery and the other half distracted by the Greelon's interruption, she failed to notice the ominous bubbles rising from the deep gorge on the other side of the coral. *Eighteen minutes.*

"I'm told drinking this beverage also improves sociability," Xstersi went on, with particular emphasis on the last word.

"Are you implying something?"

"That you prefer the solitude of frozen slush than being with other people? Heavens, no! Look here, I have an important proposition."

"I heard outsiders aren't allowed on Kazaak."

As they talked, the rising stream of bubbles

behind Jeane were plain for the Greelon to see. Unfortunately, he was oblivious to their meaning.

"You're correct. Since their *Skylar* conquerors left, the people of Kazaak have allowed no one to set foot there."

Jeane shrugged. "Uh-huh." The matter closed, she turned back to translating the coral. Her chronometer was dinging.

Xstersi persisted. "They *say* this ethanolic elixir, we can call it a beer, gets its special properties from the locals, who sing to their wheat fields. They call it *kvass*."

Damn, thought Jeane. He had her attention. "They sing to their plants?"

"Which somehow alters them." He nodded eagerly.

On far-off Earth, people were known to sing to their plants. A coincidence? Of course, no one had ever found evidence it had any effect. Still, Jeane pondered, what about the remarkable properties of this so-called kvass? Were *they* true?

"On Earth, about five centuries ago, the Duke of Bavaria decreed that beer should only be made with a grain called barley," she mused. "Of course, beer can still be made with other grains."

"Yes, yes! Surely you want to learn the secret behind the legendary Kvass of Kazaak?" he added enticingly.

She looked at him suspiciously. "What's *your* interest in this?"

"My interest?" The Greelon waved his tentacle

emphatically. "A legendary beer, notorious from the galactic center to the outer reaches from a planet no one's set foot on in more than a century, which produces a beverage which can get you smashed without a hangover?! Waddaya think? Ok, ok, I'll be honest. The *MONEY*. Every alien adolescent past the age of pubescence will be begging for it!"

Jeane grunted. "Their planet's cordoned off, so what's the point of speculating?"

Meanwhile, the bubbles behind them grew into a torrent.

"Ah, but that's where you're wrong! The people of Kazaak are opening up. They need someone with business savvy—like me to bring their product to market. And *I* need someone to verify the quality of their astonishing ale. It's a win-win for both of uh... uh... Behind—hee..." The Greelon trailed off into frightened gibberish, feebly pointing a tentacle.

Jeane looked over her shoulder.

A giant ice-shark loomed out of the gorge. Its hide was translucent like a jellyfish, yet as hard as steel. Rows of jagged teeth lined a mouth large enough to swallow a bus.

Xstersi fainted.

Jeane dived, grabbing one of his tentacles.

Jaws snapping, the ice-shark missed them by a hair's breadth. It circled back. Internal organs were dimly visible behind a single cyclopean eye which glared at her.

Her chronometer dinged. Sixteen minutes.

Holding Xstersi with her left hand, Jeane grabbed her laser cutter. She thumbed it to no effect. *Battery's drained by the cold*, she thought. *Can't cut another hole in the ice. That leaves thirty seconds to deal with the shark.* She scrambled to unholster her harpoon gun with her right hand while Xstersi floated limply in her left.

Have to get the angle just right she thought, rapidly taking aim. She held her breath as the ice-shark raced toward them.

Just a bit closer.

She pressed the trigger and pierced the ice-shark's eye. She watched breathlessly as the harpoon, visible through the shark's transparent hide, sliced through jelly-like flesh to find its mark. A tiny brain. The dead creature floated harmlessly past even as she darted upwards.

Fourteen minutes later she clambered out of the ice and hooked herself into the oxygen supply of her bubble-tent, inhaling deeply before shaking Xstersi awake. "Alright, I'll do it. But I'm doing it for the Society!"

-2-

After he revived, Xstersi promptly chartered a ship to Kazaak while Jeane packed her equipment on Cor Caroli. Soon, the nearest Astrogate had flung them through an ancient network of sentient-made wormholes across the light-years.

They dropped through pearly white clouds, and outside the passenger window Jeane saw rolling, grass-covered hills as far as the eye could see. Their vessel banked sharply and she spotted a cluster of rounded tents (it was hard to judge their size) which she guessed to be the locals' traditional habitat.

Ahead, a gleaming silver city rapidly approached. It was the only urban center on the planet with tall, spiral buildings reaching skyward like twisted knives.

Once their ship had set down, Jeane and Xstersi made for a bustling customs office where the Greelon looked around expectantly. Jeane noted they were the only off-worlders. The rest were tall, gray-skinned beings known as the *Arazi'ath* or simply, the Arazi: country dwellers seeking admission into the city. Head bowed, they passed one by one through an imposing security scanner.

"Mr. Xstersisiisterpeeze, we've been expecting you. Welcome to Kazaak!" A tall humanoid faced them. It had beady eyes like a cross between a cricket and a sardine. "Allow me to introduce myself. I am *Wort*, the envoy tasked with overseeing the kvass export deal by my government. Please." The doleful civil servant reached for Xstersi's luggage and heaved it onto a trolley. Jeane noticed he walked with a slight, painful-looking limp. The Greelon business-alien slithered after while she took up the rear.

Within the fortified city walls, each shop, each building entrance, was fitted with its own security scanner. *Awfully paranoid for a world that's supposed to be free now,* Jeane thought.

"With so few off-worlders is all this security necessary for the local population?" she asked.

"Ah? Oh, after being occupied for so long, it takes time to adjust." Wort caught Jeane's eye which had fallen on his bad leg. "A parting gift from our Masters when they released me from their..." He shrugged dismissively, casting aside the evil memory. "All that you see is just how the Skylar left it. Our people never advanced beyond the Iron Age."

Jeane didn't press him, following in respectful silence.

Finally, Wort stopped in front of a squat, warehouse-like building. "Here we are. Our brewing factory!"

-3-

Inside, they faced a series of tall copper tanks where Arazi workers were busily bottling kvass.

Wort smiled obsequiously. "Here's what you came all this way for. Ready to sample some of our famous kvass?"

"Oh, no. Not me, I can't." The Greelon pointed at his methane-water mask. "It's what *she's* here for."

"As you wish." Wort snapped his fingers. A worker hurried over.

Jeane examined the proffered glass. The liquid was a rich amber with a frothy layer on top. She took a tentative sip.

"Well?" Wort's fishy eyes were trained on her.

Jeane smacked her lips. "Excellent taste. A bit tangy, but not too much. A touch of a loafy, or bready aftertaste which is filling and..." she hesitated, but it was *so* flavorful she couldn't help adding, "...heartwarming."

Wort beamed.

"Before we proceed, you don't mind if I examine it more closely?"

The envoy bowed, pleased with her reaction.

Jeane held up the glass and passed her wrist computer over it, scanning the remaining kvass.

"So?" Xstersi asked impatiently.

"The beer's rich in nutrients. Particularly B12 and phosphorous."

"That's excellent. We can market its health benefits!"

"But it's exceptionally low in ethanol. It would be hard to get drunk on this no matter how much you drank."

Xstersi furrowed his eyestalks thoughtfully. "Kvass has a reputation all over the galaxy, so initially it'll be a big seller. As word gets around you can't get hammered, sales will drop, sure, but I'll make a mint before then!"

Jeane considered commenting on his marketing strategy, but it wasn't foremost on her mind. "I don't think you understand. Look closely at this equipment." She indicated, "Individual storage tanks with only a basic temperature gauge. No piping, no *Lauter tuns*, no cooling or conditioning tanks. It's not the usual process for making beer. Far from it. Don't you think we should investigate further? Like how they produce what you want to sell?"

"I know, I know. You want to collect cultural data for your Society. You're thinking of the legend about how they sing to their fields. Well, let me tell you. It's all bunk!"

"But what if this kvass isn't all there is? What if there's something else out there? I mean, you told me—"

"Oh, puh-lease. All you care about is your obscure obsession with galactic gastronomy!"

"It's not obscure! Beer has contributed to the building of civilizations! On my home planet, during the construction of the first great structures, pyramids, every worker got a daily ration of beer. It's the same elsewhere. Fermentation provides a safe method for storing liquids, safer than water, especially in warm climates where diseases—"

"*Yada yada*! Allow me to spell it out for you. This is all *I* need!" He turned back to Wort. "It's been a pleasure doing business. We can conclude the rest of our deal by Astrolink. Now, let's go home!"

-4-

Jeane lay in bed in the compact quarters provided by Wort, listening to Xstersi snore contentedly through his water-mask on the other side of a partition. Tomorrow, the shuttle would take them back.

Mounted on the wall, a telescreen played images of Kazaak's green hills. It was impossible to turn it off. Thankfully, the screen dimmed when the lights were out. *Can't bear to be away from their land,* Jeane thought. *Don't blame them.*

Unable to sleep, she rolled out of bed and padded to the window, pushing the curtain aside. The city walls, twelve meters high, reached right up to the windowsill. With a sigh, she looked out at the darkness beyond and the silent hills.

Jeane felt a sudden longing. How could she stay here cooped up when she hadn't learned anything? She knew she shouldn't have trusted Xstersi. He only cared about himself. How could she go back now, empty handed? She'd never get another chance. The planet was still closed to outsiders. Wort obviously wasn't telling them everything.

Jeane thought of the tents she'd seen on the flight in, not far from the city. Her mind worked quickly as she quietly dressed. When Xstersi rolled over in his sleep burbling, "No, no. Please. It tickles." Jeane stopped in her tracks, waiting until his bubbly snoring resumed. Just a Greelon dream. She didn't even want to imagine what it was.

She finished gathering her gear, snapping on her wrist computer. Recalling the security they passed through to get into the city, she knew they'd never let her out, not without permission. She'd need to think of a way to get past the guards.

Another thought struck her.

She glanced at the telescreen.

What if…

A*ll* technology here had been left by the Skylar.

As an off-worlder and therefore not to be trusted, wouldn't they want to keep an eye on her?

Jeane angled her back against the window. Yes. Out of view of the telescreen. She tested the strength of the curtains. The window was three meters across. She silently pulled down the curtain and cut it into four strips. That gave her twelve meters. She tied the ends together.

Sliding out the window on her makeshift rope and over the wall, she promised herself she'd be back in time for the morning shuttle.

-5-

A circular tent loomed out of the dark. It had taken Jeane an hour to reach it, tramping across the damp, open grass. Fifty more spread out behind it like mushrooms in a field.

She wasn't sure what to expect. If it *was* a village, she hoped to find someone about. She could ask a few questions. All part of being a good Chef Hunter, a good detective.

Even from a distance she could tell the tent city didn't sleep. Tall lights posted around it glared harshly on white canvas. A cacophonous mix of speech and music disturbed the silent night.

A festival of some kind? Yet, there was a hardness to the words and an artificiality to the music, combined with the starkness of the light. Something wasn't right.

Jeane prudently approached the nearest structure from behind, glancing between a row of tents.

Halfway down the lane a large telescreen was mounted on struts.

Jeane thought about the heavy security to get in and these ubiquitous telescreens. *Don't like how it's adding up.*

She put her ear to the tent. Muffled sounds.

She crawled to the opening and lifted the flap.

Arazi, maybe twenty, were crammed onto benches staring blearily at yet another telescreen.

"Fellows! For too long have you been kept down by the Out-Worlders!" The strident voice was accompanied by images of workers in a field. "Soon, your labor and your self-sacrifice will bear fruit. By your toil, by your sweat, we will rise up as one glorious people. Our hour is upon us. But we must keep working! We must never cease! We must never tire!"

The voice reached a crescendo. "Our supreme leader, *Big Didi*, will lead us to greatness! Under Big Didi we will have a glorious future!"

-6-

One of the Arazi lolled on his seat half-asleep, about to fall over.

"You there! Lazing! Don't you want to be part of our great Fellowship? Comrades, wake him! Slap him if you have to! That's it. Harder!"

So, the screen could see you.

Jeane backed away carefully, lowering the tent flap.

An indoctrination camp, she realized. She felt a pang of disgust. But what could she do? The Society's motto was to *Serve and Preserve*. She wasn't here to interfere. She had her own job to do.

Jeane pondered her next move.

Where could she go to learn more about kvass without being discovered? She knew she didn't have much time when she heard voices.

"Too good for us, eh? Don't want to do your part? You don't see us shirking our duties, do you?"

Jeane cautiously poked her head around the corner of the tent.

Two gray-skinned Arazi, one tall and broad and the other shorter, carrying metal pikestaffs, prodded along a third with olive-green skin.

"Alright, that's far enough," commanded the tall one. "It'll only take a minute. Then you'll be *just like us*. No escaping it now. We're not primitives anymore, are we?"

"You're nothing but... insects!" their prisoner spat defiantly, breaking away. It was a female.

She was steps away from Jeane's hiding spot when the shorter Arazi caught up and swung his pikestaff. A long pole, its tip crackling with electricity like a cattle prod, hit her squarely between the shoulders. She fell to her knees.

"Stinkin' *Rider*!" the short one bellowed. "We'll clip you good!"

Jeane flattened herself on the grass. The female Arazi sprawled breathless, doubled up in pain, just a few feet away. A small pair of wings reflexively unfurled from her back; they didn't look large enough to support flight. The short guard grabbed a wing tip and yanked.

The female cried out.

"You can make all the noise you want, but we're still gonna clip you!" he snarled as he activated a laser cutter which he loosened from his belt.

The red beam hummed dangerously.

"Stop moving!"

The tall one quickly caught up and shoved his pikestaff into her back. She writhed in agony.

"We've all got to do it sometime," the tall one expounded, "so just hold still. We can't go into space–we can't fit into our spacesuits–with those wings, can we?"

"Stop blabbering and hold her down! I don't wanna cut my hand."

The tall one pressed harder on his pikestaff which hissed angrily. Smoke rose from her back. "Just think of it as cutting off... the *past*. Don't need them decorative appendages anymore. We've outgrown them. Big Didi said so."

Jeane couldn't stand by any longer. But what to do? *Something had better come to me* she thought. "Hello? What's going on?" She stood up.

The guards stopped in mid-action, glaring at her with beady eyes.

"Who're you?" the guard holding the laser growled.

A plan formulated in her mind. "They didn't tell you?" *Time to gamble*. "I'm sure you heard about the kvass export deal with the off-worlders? Hard to miss the ship that came in today."

The guards nodded slowly, unsure what to do. Just as she hoped.

"Big Didi sent me to check on your telescreens. They don't fix themselves, do they? You realize, over time, they run down. But I'm sure you knew that since you know all about technology."

The two guards looked at each other wondering what to do. The mere mention of *Big Didi* made them hesitate.

"Whoa," she shouted before they had time to think, "your laser's out of phase! Pass it here. Quick! I can fix it."

The short one wavered—and uncertainly

handed it over.

"Thanks." Jeane turned the laser on his pikestaff, on the battery charger at its base. With a loud *bang* the pikestaff exploded and the two Arazi fell to the ground.

She hurried to check on them. They were stunned but not dead, to her relief.

Which is when she heard the hum of the laser cutter she'd cast aside at her throat.

-7-

"All packed?"

Wort stood in the open doorway, bright morning sunlight glaring at his back.

"It's been a very productive trip." Xstersi plopped his suitcase down at the envoy's feet. Wort forced a thin smile.

"Jeane, our ride's here!" Xstersi called over his shoulder. He followed Wort out the door, repeating impatiently, "Jeane!" When there was no reply he stopped, "Jeane?" He looked at Wort. "Just a minute."

He rapped a tentacle on the partition dividing their sleeping quarters. "Jeane, what's taking you so long? Our shuttle's waiting."

Silence.

He put his tentacles on his hip-joints. "Jeane! Is this supposed to be some kind of a joke! Really, you don't have a funny bone in your non-chitinous body. Do you see me laughing?"

Still nothing.

As he didn't hear so much as a peep on the other side, he stole a glance round the partition with his eyestalks. "Yoo-hoo, Jeane?"

He saw her empty, unmade bed, her travel bag, and an open window.

Oh, no! She's gone... To find out more about the kvass, I bet! She's gonna ruin me.

Xstersi slithered back to Wort, his three brains working overtime.

"Hey." He grinned sheepishly.

Wort stared at him with black, unblinking eyes.

"Well now," Xstersi began, racking his three brains for a way to explain the situation without jeopardizing their deal, "ah, er... it seems... my zythological assistant... uh..." And then it came to him, the obvious, devious answer. "She can't hold her kvass! That's it! She's out like a light! Hungover."

"But—"

"Humans are pretty weak, you know. Up all night, barfing!" He grimaced, making an ugly face. "All night, she was–gah–oof–blah! Vomit everywhere. Can't wake her now, sorry."

"But what do I tell my superiors?" Wort whined.

"We'll take the next shuttle. Simple." Xstersi reached a tentacle out and yanked his bag back in. "See yah!" He slammed the door in Wort's face. And prayed to the Gods of Greelon that Jeane Oberon would turn up soon.

-8-

Jeane trekked through short, dry grass with the Arazi female at her back, laser cutter turned off to preserve power but at the ready should she try to make a run for it.

Behind them the backs of telescreens stood out on lonely hilltops against the azure sky.

The Arazi had taken Jeane hostage to ensure safe passage back to—where? Jeane wasn't sure. And what would happen when they reached their destination?

What will she do with me then?

They hadn't spoken during the long night's march. After the explosion (of the pike staff), the female ordered Jeane into a ditch and gave brief instructions to throw off their pursuers. They'd crawled most of the night through the hollows between hills, avoiding the eyes of the ever-present telescreens.

They'd left the last one in the distance hours ago.

Working the stiffness out of her joints—she'd been up for more than a day now—Jeane reflected. Maybe it wasn't so bad being hostage. Like having a guide. She didn't know where they were going, but it had to be somewhere she could learn more about the secrets of kvass, right?

Before setting out for Kazaak, Jeane had read all the documentation the Skylar had gathered, however limited. *And there are still a few things I can try, to learn even more*, she thought.

Ahead, the green feet of the mountains rose into higher gray peaks. They were at least a day's march away.

"Are we going to those mountains?" she asked. "How long will it take?"

No answer.

Have to get her to open up.

"So, they force you to cultivate the fields to enrich Big Didi. Is that how it is?"

The Arazi trudged on in stony silence.

"Ok, you don't have to answer. You do recall I saved you, though?"

The Arazi scowled. "They think they can make themselves into Out-Worlders like *you*. Big Didi hides himself, his face, like a worm. Just as the Skylar did. He looks up too much at the stars."

"What do you plan to do with me?"

The Arazi hesitated. She growled, "Feed you to the Massif!"

Surprisingly, Jeane laughed and shook her head. "I don't think so, whatever the Massif is."

"Oh, no?"

"I've watched you. You're not like them."

Her captor turned away, grumbling, "They've kept me in their camp too long. I'm not what I was."

"Don't worry yourself. I'm not that easy to get rid of."

But the female just ignored her and stopped, glancing from side to side, sniffing the air. Her small wings reflexively uncurled and just as quickly folded back against her body, as if in anticipation.

Jeane felt the ground shake.

Then it became more tremulous. Earthquake?

She rubbed her eyes. The land ahead was moving. As if a green wave had rolled under, lifted up the grass and set it down again!

The Arazi raised her arms and let out a shrill musical shout.

Listening to the trilling, Jeane momentarily forgot the land itself was bearing down on them in a roiling tsunami. *The singing!*

She turned back and saw two undulating, churning green lines. And riding the crest of each was an Arazi! Jeane remembered: the guards had called their prisoner a *Rider*. But a rider of what?

She held her breath.

The heaving ground abruptly flattened, depositing the Arazi. Each held some kind of leather sled–or was it more like a saddle?

Jeane excitedly bent to her knees, running her hand through the grass. Completely intact. No sign anything had dug through. How could something have burrowed under the ground and left it untouched, pristine?

"Urumqi!" the riders joyfully shouted, running to embrace Jeane's captor. "We feared you'd been clipped! We've been tending the Massif."

Urumqi turned her gaze on Jeane. "This one helped me." Tall and proud she walked up, eye-to-eye. "I release you. Go." She pointed back the way they had come. "Return to your stars. Speak to the first telescreen you come across. They will come for you. We will be long gone."

Jeane replied, "I was thinking I could go on. With you."

"Go? Where? To spy on us?"

"No. I'd like to learn about—"

"This is why you saved me? To follow us back?" She pointed angrily. "You must go!"

Jeane thought, *time to play my final card.* "In that case I demand… Trial by Kvass!"

Urumqi's olive-green face slowly turned black with anger as her words sunk in. "You can't! I refuse your challenge!"

"She has the right, Urumqi." One of the riders stepped up. "You can't refuse Trial by Kvass."

Urumqi looked ready to boil over. Instead, she roughly grabbed a saddle-sled, singing shrilly. Her wings unfurled and flapped with a phosphorous light. She threw the saddle on the ground. "Very well!" She pushed Jeane onto it.

The ground rose up.

-9-

Jeane sped across the snaking landscape past curving, gray peaks. She clung to the saddle-sled with Urumqi behind her, their legs dangling over—what?

Glancing over her shoulder she saw Urumqi's faintly luminescent wings rattling in the wind like sails. For balance? Every now and again the Arazi let out a shrill cry, altering their direction.

The rolling ground propelled them onward as if they were perched on the tip of a green wave. It was breathtaking.

At last they stopped in front of two solitary tents pitched among the verdant hills. Again, Jeane ran her hand through the damp grass. Just like the soil on a hundred other planets. *What is it?*

"Wait here," Urumqi commanded. She leaned her saddle-sled against a tent and went in.

The circular tents were traditional Arazi *yurts*. The roof of the nearer was extended on a short pole to vent the day's heat. Stepping closer, Jeane saw they were both carefully tied to the grass, unlike those by the city which had spikes driven into the ground.

To the left, a rusting moss-covered hover bike

was parked. Presumably stolen from the Skylar. In front was an oven made of sun-dried bricks. Pleasant smelling charcoal smoke wafted from it. Flat breads, browned and crusty, were stacked at its feet.

An elderly Arazi'ath, shriveled like a dried prune, beat long, bronze stalks of grass against the side of the oven. A type of rye grain, Jeane observed, *Secale Cereale.*

Jeane thought, *grain for bread, and grain for beer!* She studied the old woman. *What's your connection to this strange land?* But before she could formulate a question the crone spoke.

"You come from Skylar? Skylar always cover face. I never see. Your face, is face of Skylar?"

"No. I'm not Skylar."

"Good. Skylar are insects!" the wrinkled creature spat.

"To tell you the truth, I've often felt the same way," Jeane said. "One of the Overseers of my Society happens to be Skylar. He sometimes refuses to finance my expeditions. Still, they're not all like you remember. Times change."

The old Arazi shook her head. "All Skylar are trash! I mop blood from their *room.* Where they try to break us. Break our mind!"

"Must have been a long time ago."

"No, not so long. After they go, I clean blood from same room. For *our* Big Didi. He also insect! First Skylar break him! Next he wants to *be* Skylar!"

She's seen Big Didi?

Jeane asked a few questions and was deep in thought when Urumqi stomped out, scowling. "You will come inside now!"

-10-

Within, Jeane saw the yurt was decorated with wall hangings. Dusty carpets covered the floor with delicate designs of flowers in hues of sky blue, purple and pink. A table with a white tablecloth stitched with arabesques occupied the middle of the tent. There were no chairs. On either side lay two rough-hewn drinking cups.

The old crone followed them in.

Jeane put all questions of Big Didi out of her mind. It wasn't her responsibility, she told herself. *This* was what she was here for.

In the corner was a large steaming pot. The crone shuffled over carrying a handful of flat breads. With her bare hands she broke them and opened the pot, filled with boiling water, and let the crouton like chunks spill in. "Mmm, just a bit of *zakvaska.*"

The loafy smell that escaped was unmistakable. Kvass!

Of course! Why had she assumed the Arazi's beer needed complicated brewing machinery? All they had to do was let their rye bread ferment in boiling water which would naturally result in a beer like drink.

Still, one burning question remained.

Did they sing to their wheat fields like the riders had sung to the churning land and whatever creature lay beneath?

And if so, what effect did it have?

Jeane hoped to find out.

Everything depended on the Trial.

Urumqi strode purposefully in and picked a large ceramic jug off the floor from next to the steaming brewing pot. She placed it in the center of the table between the two cups.

"We can begin, elder Aunt," she said.

The old Arazi uncapped the jug. "Our Urumqi is a champion drinker! You know our rules?"

Jeane nodded. "If I win you must give me anything I ask for."

"And if you lose, we will feed you to the Massif," growled Urumqi, "because this is what I will ask for."

Fat chance, thought Jeane. *She doesn't know that kvass is low in ethanol. And its other digestive properties don't affect humans.*

The old woman filled the cups. "Whoever falls first, loses."

Urumqi brought a cup to her lips, tilted her head majestically, and gulped it down.

Glaring defiantly, she slammed the cup on the table.

Jeane held her own cup under her nose. There was a light foam on top and unlike the dark amber of the kvass from the factory this beer was practically glowing golden yellow.

"Well, here goes nothing." She took a swig.

The bubbly liquid flowed over her tongue. *Now, that's the real deal! Liquid bread. I've never tasted anything like it!*

And then—the room swam. Her knees buckled. She put a hand on the table, steadying herself.

"Please, your hand. Not allowed," Urumqi's aunt warned.

Jeane quickly withdrew her arm, realizing she'd made a terrible mistake.

Why had she assumed all kvass was the same? That's two false assumptions in a row, she told herself. *This kvass is loaded with neurotransmission interfering ethanol and who knows what else?*

The old crone smiled, refilling the cups.

Urumqi downed her second beer. Rock steady.

Ok, Jeane. You can still do this. Breathe. She drank her second cup and closed her eyes.

Opened them.

Saw Urumqi put down the third cup.

Jeane drank her next cup. Then her fourth. And a fifth.

Smiled. Felt so happy.

She felt the ground totter. *That thing! It's under the ground again.* She looked down at her feet, but they were *soooo* far away. *No! If I just sit for a bit.*

Something inside told her not to. "Your turn!"

Urumqi shook her head throwing off her own cobwebs.

It's getting to her.

The Arazi drank a sixth cup but it took two laborious swallows to finish.

Jeane's throat constricted and her eyes watered. She wiped them. Everything was blurry.

She held the sixth beer to her lips, but her mouth refused to open. *Must drink!*

Urumqi watched her from across the table with inscrutable black eyes.

The old woman looked at Jeane. "You finished? No more?"

Jeane mastered herself and held her head back, letting the golden liquid froth down her throat. It dribbled down her chin.

Urumqi's aunt looked at her in wonder. "Six cups! No one's ever gone past six!" She turned uncertainly to Urumqi, who resolutely nodded for her to continue.

She poured them each a seventh cup.

Sound exploded in the room and Jeane felt everything spin. Suddenly, she was staring at blue sky. There were children's voices. How had she gotten outside? Was it over? No, she was just looking out the tent's open roof. She looked down. Still standing.

Half-a-dozen Arazi children scampered about the tent. Behind them, just entering, Jeane recognized the two Arazi she'd encountered earlier.

As if from underwater she heard, "We woke the kids from their midday rest to witness your great feat, Urumqi!"

"Big sister!" A leaf-green child wrapped tiny arms around Urumqi's leg.

Slowly Urumqi raised her seventh beer and guzzled it down.

The children cheered, making strange throat sounds.

They then turned to Jeane making faces, waving their arms, and flapping little wings, doing everything and anything to make Jeane dizzier than she already was. The room whirled like a spinning top.

The old female chided them, "Stop that! Cut it out! The contest must be fair!"

The kids ignored her, chanting, stamping their feet, and sticking out their green tongues.

Unfortunately for them it had the opposite effect. *They're so adorable,* Jeane thought as she drank the seventh cup.

She set it down and as her gaze fell across the table, she noticed something curious. Urumqi was standing right up next to it. In fact, she was leaning against the table for support.

Jeane pointed. "Elder Aunt… isn't… isn't that… against… rules?"

"Yes. Urumqi, what're you doing? Please, step back!"

But Urumqi made no effort to move. She just stared ahead into empty space.

Her aunt tapped her waist where she was leaning against the table to gently push her away, and Urumqi fell backwards like a statue.

"Wah!" the children wailed.

"I... I would like..." Jeane mumbled, "as my prize... to see you sing to your fields... right after... after... a little nap."

-11-

Jeane was gently prodded awake by the old Arazi'ath. Curled up on the carpeted floor, she rubbed her eyes and looked around. She was in a strange tent. Where was she? Then it came back. She put her hand to her throbbing temple and stood, testing her legs. Her head quickly cleared. Remarkable. Just like Xstersi had said. No hangover! She followed the old crone outside.

Night had fallen.

Urumqi was waiting. "It is time for what you ask," she sighed reluctantly, and Jeane wondered if she was breaking some taboo, some sacred ritual by asking to see the Arazi sing. Was it forbidden to outsiders? *What does it mean to them?* She'd come all this way to find out.

Urumqi guided her through the cool night.

They reached a rounded hill and stopped at its base. Wind blew through the long grass rustling expectantly at their feet. Glancing up the slope, Jeane saw tall silver grains quivering and dancing in the moonlight. The air was malt scented.

After a time in hushed silence Jeane looked around and saw that others had joined them. They wavered like the long stalks of grain, softly rocking in the breeze.

It started with a barely audible whisper from Urumqi. Her eyes were closed.

At some unseen cue, the others joined in. Their song broke the silent night. How to describe a sound you've never heard before? The music was deep, like the roots of the mountains and as soft as a single note on a reed.

Jeane wanted to close her eyes to let it wash over her, but she reminded herself she was here to document, to collect every detail. She activated her wrist computer to record it.

Urumqi passionately, mournfully, sang to the hill with her upturned face.

Then, when Jeane thought the apex could reach no higher, Urumqi's wings unfurled, exploding with color!

Light enveloped the hillside. The very veins of the Arazi's wings glowed with swirling, phosphorous hues. Blue, emerald, gold. Pulses of light reverberated far off into the night.

Initially Jeane recorded without thought, in awe. Then she forced her mind to observe more closely to put order to it, to understand the alien ritual. How did all the pieces of the puzzle fit together? Where did the kvass fit in? The singing? The land, and what lay beneath? The Riders? They were all connected, but by what thread? She recalled the word 'ale' which in Old English held connotations of sorcery and magic.

For a brief moment Jeane thought, here among

the stars, I've found something.

Then the ground trembled.

The thing under the earth. They've summoned it.

She heard a high-pitched whistle in the air far above her head, and the song broke off.

Strange. It sounds more like an incoming—

The explosion knocked her off her feet. Black smoke drifted across the stars.

The shaking of the ground was joined by a mechanical *whirr*. Jeane looked up. A formation of tanks rolled over the top of the hill. Arazi soldiers wearing black goggles sat between earth-churning steel treads.

Designed to dig up the ground. To tear into it.

To subdue what lay beneath.

A voice called over a megaphone, "Fellows! You know you're not allowed to congregate! Big Didi has forbidden it!"

The Arazi ran.

Heat rolled across Jeane accompanied by the smell of burning grass. *The grain!*

No, they weren't aiming at it, wouldn't intentionally damage the government's cash cow, it was just collateral damage. The blasts weren't even aimed at the Arazi, but rather—

"They're encircling us!" Urumqi shouted.

They were firing well over the Arazi's heads. Herding them. Preventing the Riders from escaping on their mysterious steeds.

The megaphone continued over the booms, "Big Didi said we must destroy *all* old ideas! *All* old customs! *All* old habits! Fellows, look to the future! We must all be clipped!"

The single-manned tanks broke formation, fanning out. Troops goose stepping behind leveled pikestaffs at the frightened Arazi.

Jeane observed. The encircling bombardment appeared haphazard. The equipment left by the Skylar wasn't that advanced. And yet, she wasn't sure how precise they could be.

"We can't go back! Push through their line of fire. It's our only chance!" she hollered.

Urumqi understood at once. They ducked their heads and took their chances amid a hail of earth-shaking detonations.

Bits of sod flew through the air. Rained down. Jeane looked back. The others were being corralled with sharp jabs from pikestaffs onto a primitive, flat-bed hovercraft.

Turning to check ahead she saw the faint, far off glimmer of a telescreen.

Oh, no! It must've picked up the Arazi's light! That's why Urumqi didn't want me to see the ritual. She knew it wasn't safe. Why didn't she warn me? Jeane shook her head, but she knew the answer. Trial Bound.

They ran for their lives.

"Can't you call for your mounts?" Jeane yelled breathlessly as they sprinted.

"The Massif won't respond. Not with these discharges," Urumqi shouted back.

Jeane reviewed their plight. The tanks were

closing in. They couldn't outrun them, and the bombardment was getting closer. *What if they don't care if they blast us to bits,* she thought desperately.

Urumqi came to the same conclusion. "We can't escape!"

She kneeled close to the earth and Jeane saw her softly sing, mouth to the ground, golden wings unfurled.

Suddenly, the ground opened at Jeane's feet and she stumbled into a yawning gap. She felt something push her down, envelop her. It felt sticky and grass-like, pinning her. She struggled not to panic, but it was too heavy. She was being smothered!

Through a tiny gap she saw Urumqi's face, close. "Maybe *you* can save us," she breathed in Jeane's ear.

In another heartbeat the soldiers surrounded Urumqi. A dozen pikestaffs converged, crackling with electricity. She writhed in pain.

The last thing Jeane saw was Urumqi's limp form being dragged to the prisoner craft.

Then the ground enfolded her, and everything went black.

-12-

Xstersi was fretfully pacing in their hotel room leaving a pale trail of nervous slime. "It's all gonna unravel. The deal of a lifetime. Where are you, Jeane?!" He glanced anxiously out the window for the umpteenth time. Having spotted earlier the curtains she had used to climb out, he had pulled them up and left them piled on the floor hoping no one had noticed them.

The long night had painfully ticked by minute by minute stretching him to the breaking point. By morning, his nerves were shot and he eyed, not for the first time, the complimentary bottle of kvass, gleaming golden brown, sitting on the glass coffee table.

"What did she say about it? Doesn't interfere with brain functioning? But increases positive feelings?"

He finally gave in and popped the cap off. "My three brains can certainly use a dose of dopamine!" He pressed a button on his breathing mask and the liquid methane in it gurgled into the tank on his back. His faceplate hissed open. Xstersi chug-a-lugged the kvass.

When his faceplate had clicked back into place and been replenished, he mused, "Hmmm, not bad. Tastes just like rotten Quibble eggs. My favorite!" He burped and screwed up his eyes.

After a moment, he put a tentacle to his forehead and reflected, "That... that scheming, deceitful human female! She neglected to tell me how the kvass affects Greelons, on purpose, no doubt. I'm drunk!"

The doorbell rang.

"Oh no!"

Xstersi slunk across the room, his tentacles splayed in all directions as if he was aboard a ship in heavy seas. He fumbled to find the door fob.

Finally, the door slid open. Xstersi's eyestalks drooped. He had to exert himself to look up at Wort, waiting impatiently in the hall. "Heh. Hiya... Hip!"

"I hope your assistant is fully recovered?"

"Ah... about that." Xstersi felt the room tilt.

"Are you alright?"

"Oh, yes. Fine. Lying down on one's guest is a Greelon sign of respect."

"Do you need a hand?"

"No, no, don't trouble yourself." Xstersi hauled himself across the floor, onto the couch. Wort followed him in.

"Are you ready to go?"

"Uhn." Xstersi struggled to think straight, but his three brains felt like they had been tied in a knot. "Yes, well, uhm... Jeane decided to do a little last minute… uh, souvenir hunting. I tried to tell her it wasn't the time." He waved a tentacle vaguely.

"Souvenir shopping? Where?"

"Oof! That telescreen! So bright. My eyestalks are throbbing! Can't you shut if off?" He closed his eyes and his eyestalks fell limp.

"I'm sorry, there's nothing I can do. Mr. Xstersisiisterpeeze? Are you sleeping?"

Just then Wort heard a voice from the open window. He snapped his head around.

"Xstersi! Are you there? It's me, Jeane."

The Greelon's eyes popped open. "Oh, sh—"

"Xstersi! It's me."

"Gah! Cough!" the Greelon spluttered.

"Did you hear that?" Wort asked.

"What? I only hear the wind and it's giving me a headache! I'm gonna close the window. If I can just… just… get up."

"I was sure I heard—"

"Xstersi!"

The Greelon blabbered over the sound of Jeane's voice, "Oh, I'm burning up! Fetch me a glass of water! In all haste! Hurry, or I'm gonna be sick."

"I thought Greelons didn't drink?"

"To dip my tentacles in! Quickly, you imbecile! Ah! There, I've gone and spilled my ink."

A sticky, black puddle pooled on the floor. Wort skirted around it and made for the window.

Sticking his head out he saw Jeane at the base of the wall next to a rusted hover bike.

She didn't appear surprised to see the envoy. "Wort! You're just the person I was looking for! Check near your feet. Xstersi must've put the curtains I tied up there. Throw them down, so I can climb up."

After a moment's hesitation, presumably deciding if he should help her or not, Wort threw down the makeshift rope. Jeane clambered up and Wort held out his hand, helping her into the room. She was covered head-to-toe with a fibrous brown grass clinging to her hair and skin.

With expressionless eyes Wort watched Jeane go to the sink and wipe her face.

Xstersi, meanwhile, squashed himself into the couch as if to make himself invisible. He peered nervously over the rim with his eyestalks.

Jeane returned, leaving the sink running noisily. She pulled in the curtains from the window. "Looks like Xstersi got ink all over these."

Seeing that they were in fact spotless, Wort objected, "No, they're perfectly—"

Jeane put a finger to her lips. She casually draped the curtains over the telescreen. Next, she took off her wrist computer and placed it near the screen's base, her recorded observations of coral on Cor Caroli playing loudly.

Wort watched with an inscrutable expression. Jeane knew she was taking an awful risk, especially after what she'd learned.

"By the Gods of Greelon, where have you been? What's going on?" Xstersi blurted, unable to keep silent any longer.

"I believe Wort knows what the precautions are for," Jeane said.

The envoy nodded slowly. He seemed ready to listen, so she continued. "As for where I've been, that's a long story. More importantly, I've learned that the native population is being rounded up. Into forced labor camps. I only just escaped myself thanks to, I guess they call it the Massif, which hid me. It released me when the coast was clear, and I went to make sure some Arazi children I'd met were safe. There was a hover bike near their tent which I borrowed to get here."

"She's mad! Don't listen to her," Xstersi cut in abruptly, "she only cares about the legend of the kvass!"

"You're right," Jeane rounded angrily on him. "I made a mess of it. I was only thinking of myself. Because of my obsession I've put others in danger. I was blind to... to the fact that other people are important to me too."

Xstersi's eyestalks opened wide in amazement. He wasn't sure what he felt. Was it *sympathy*? Jeane admitted making a mistake. His retort got stuck in his throat-sac. He was speechless.

"What do you want from me?" Wort asked in the subdued silence that followed.

"I remember what you said when we first landed," Jeane answered. "I believe, because of what the Skylar did to you, you don't agree with Big Didi's plan." She inhaled deeply, hoping she was on the right track and plunged on. "I need to find a friend, and you're the only one who can help."

For a long moment Wort said nothing, his alien face impossible to read. Xstersi looked apprehensively from Jeane to the envoy. What was he thinking? Would he turn them in?

At length Wort nodded. "Alright, I'll do what I can. If you'll follow me."

Jeane smiled, relieved. *It might work.*

"Wait! What do I do?" Xstersi wailed, afraid to be left alone again.

Jeane snatched up her wrist computer and turned off the recording. She tossed it to the Greelon who deftly caught it, all sobered up.

"Listen to my findings," she said.

"Your findings? Who cares?"

"Listen to them," Jeane ordered with such finality it made Xstersi sit up as she followed Wort out the door.

In the corridor, Wort stopped and thoughtfully turned to her once more. "I just have one last question," he asked slowly. "Did you really think I'd turn on my own government, on Big Didi, when I *am* Big Didi!"

At some unseen signal, Jeane was surrounded by a dozen Arazi soldiers, their pikestaffs leveled at her and crackling terrifyingly.

-13-

Wort (that is, Big Didi) stood patiently with his hands behind his back.

Jeane lay flat on her back, unconscious, on a metal table with a strange bar extending over her forehead. Behind Wort was a large telescreen, but unlike other screens this one had knobs and buttons along its base, though it was currently blank.

Jeane's eyes fluttered. She slowly rolled her head to the side.

"Awake? You had a terrible shock. Many, many shocks in fact."

Her eyes flared, but she didn't move.

"It will take some time for your strength to return."

"What do you plan to do with us?" she grunted.

"I require the Greelon for his access to galactic markets, but he doesn't have a clue, in so many ways. I don't think he'll be a problem. As for you, you've been uncovering things you shouldn't, causing trouble, and getting others into trouble too. Your friend Urumqi is scheduled for this room as soon as we're done here. A hard nut to crack that one. Almost as hard as you. The children you met in the hills will be brought in for re-education as well. So, you see, it's just as you said. You really messed things up. Not for me of course, but for your friends. Oh, you look unhappy now."

"Then, why am I still here?"

"I presume you mean why are you still alive? I'm told you and your Galactic Culinary Society —whoever heard of such a thing by the way— are something of a celebrity. It would be noticed if you suddenly disappeared. I'd rather not have Intergalactic Peacekeepers nosing around."

Jeane turned away from him. "You're pathetic."

Ignoring her comment, Wort tapped the bar over her forehead. "This is a neural immobilizer. The Skylar didn't like watching their victims thrashing about making a mess, foaming at the mouth, soiling themselves, what have you. Quite simply, they didn't believe it was the *civilized* way to torture someone."

He licked his lips with suppressed lasciviousness. "The device induces extreme pain, to the point of erasing memory. I have a few holes in my mind too, I do. Oh, but you never forget the pain. Anyway, once we're all done here, you'll be sent on your way with the Greelon and we'll be none the worse for it. No, don't try to get up. You won't be able to."

Jeane's head sank back down. "You can't control everything."

"Mmm. You've seen our telescreens?" He waved

to the large screen on the wall. Blank, it dully reflected his tall, gangly shape. "The screens have a hypnotic power over the populace. I suppose it's because we're new to technology. If we'd grown up with it like you have, I'm sure we could resist its mind-numbing allure."

He pulled a lever on the bar over her head. "We'll start with the lowest setting, shall we? You will feel—just feel, mind you, it's all happening in your head—you will feel screws slowly being twisted into your skull. It should start about now. When we're done, your memory of kvass—the real one, the one you shared with your friend out there, the most fantastic beverage to be found anywhere in the universe—will be wiped clean from your mind. If you should ever come across a glass of kvass again, though I doubt you will, you will find it utterly *tasteless*."

He observed her with his black unblinking eyes. She didn't so much as twitch.

"Let's turn it up. This mid-setting is usually sufficient to produce the desired result. I don't think I've ever needed to set it to maximum."

Pacing near her, he lay a gray hand on her leg. "You'll now feel your wings slowly, very slowly, being ripped from your body. Even Arazi who've been clipped claim they feel phantom wings being torn. Ah, but I'm forgetting. You're human. You don't have wings. I'm not sure what you'll feel. Well, it must be excruciatingly painful. Do you know, it was the Skylar who first discovered that clipping an Arazi's wings leaves them dead inside?"

He circled indulgently to give her a better view of his scarred, wingless back.

"The only thing that's painful right now," Jeane said through gritted teeth, "is having to listen to you. It's worse than listening to Xstersi."

Wort quivered with rage. He'd never faced resistance before. Flecks of spit flew from his mouth. "In that case, you won't mind if I just set it to maximum!"

-14-

Big Didi slash Wort angrily strode out, knowing it would take time and an incredible amount of pain to erase Jeane's memory.

He returned a little later, approaching the table where she lay immobile, eyes closed. Her breathing was shallow as if asleep. Wort stepped closer, studying her curiously. There were no external signs on her body. How effective had the device been on the human?

Her chest rose and fell rhythmically. Had she been put into a coma? Perhaps setting it to maximum had been a mistake.

Tink! Tink!

A sound like someone tapping on glass interrupted his line of thought. He turned and saw the Greelon staring at him from the telescreen.

"Who left that on?" Wort demanded.

"That would be me." Jeane sat up, perfectly alert. "Is everything ready, Xstersi?"

The Greelon held up his tentacle. "I've plugged your wrist computer into the system."

Wort's mouth fell open. "This can't be."

Jeane slid easily off the table. "Unfortunately,

you made the assumption that this Skylar device designed for Arazi would also work on humans. But we don't have the same physiognomy. And by unfortunately, I mean unfortunately for you."

"It had no effect?!"

Jeane smiled. "Don't beat yourself up about it. I've made a few false assumptions lately too. So, to be sure, I checked up on how the Skylar occupied various planets before letting myself fall into your hands."

"You… *let*? You knew who I was?"

"Urumqi's aunt used to work for you and your bad leg tipped me off. Her description was unmistakable. I asked her a few questions and she described *this* room to me in detail."

Wort's eyes darkened. "A room you won't escape from."

Jeane was nonplussed. "Uh-huh. When she said the room had a telescreen with controls on it, I knew I had to get in here, one way or the other."

"What benefit would that be to you? Other than an untimely death?"

Jeane turned to the telescreen by way of answer. "Xstersi, activate program one-nine-eight-four."

The Greelon pressed a button on Jeane's wrist computer, plugged into the telescreen in their hotel room.

She explained, "According to Urumqi's aunt you left prisoners unattended. Of course, I couldn't know what you'd do with me, but it was a risk worth taking. Worst case scenario, I figured I could overpower you to hack into your private telescreen here. As it is, you very kindly left me enough time to access all the telescreens everywhere on the planet."

"You believe sending some message to the populace to rise up against me will work? Ha! How foolish can you be?!"

"My signal isn't for the people. It's for the Massif. Well, the Massifs. They're semi-sentient, fungal-plant creatures. So large, only a few hundred cover the entire surface of Kazaak. Each one is hundreds of kilometers in size.

"They've evolved a symbiotic relationship with your kind. Arazi cultivate the Massif's grass-like epidermis and direct mobile root systems to sources of water, like shepherds. In return, the Massif provides transportation on its roots and offers sustenance from an overabundance of seedlings. I'm sending instructions to the Massif. All of them."

Music began playing on the telescreen similar to what Jeane had heard Urumqi sing. The same deep melancholic dirge, but somehow more hopeful, accompanied by flashing, multi-colored lights which replaced Xstersi's image.

"It's my own composition," Jeane nodded proudly, "based on my studies of the ritual."

Suddenly Wort sprang forward, fast even with his bad leg, and pressed the mute button before Jeane could get to him. The lights continued soundlessly.

"So much for your message!" he barked triumphantly.

"In point of fact," Jeane said, "it's not the song which the Massif hears. Plants obviously don't have auditory receptors." While she talked, she swiftly grabbed Wort's arm and twisted it behind his back before he could reach any other controls. "Of course, the Arazi sing anyway, but it's more like how my species, humans, use gestures and facial expressions without really thinking about it. Actually, the Arazi communicate through *photomorphogenesis*. The Massif, like all plants, has photoreceptors which capture light energy. Phytochrome pigments respond to reds and chlorophylls absorb the blue end of the electromagnetic spectrum."

She directed him to the metal table. With a forceful thrust and turn, Wort was on his back. He eyed the bar over his head. His whole body stiffened, going rigid with fear.

"Don't worry," Jeane said, "I don't believe in an eye for an eye. I'll just activate the immobilizer, which *will* work on *you*."

She tapped him good-naturedly on the chest. "Now, as I was saying, on my planet, a man named Darwin documented plant responses to blue light, oh, a long time ago. And more recently, we've discovered how to control plant growth with colored lights. We can change the size, texture, even flavors with different light inputs and..." she sighed, realizing she was getting off track. "Xstersi was right. I am obsessed with arcane things! Anyway, what I'm trying to say is this: Arazi sing with their wings."

On the telescreen behind her, golds and blues, reds and greens pulsed with a psychedelic rhythm.

She continued, "All the ingredients for kvass come from the Massif. The beer contains a ton of phosphorus which powers the chemiluminescence in your–ah, I'm forgetting, you don't have any–in the wings of your people. A powerful example of the virtuous circle of nature, don't you think? Hmm. Now *you* don't look happy."

When she finished speaking the radiant light which had played all over the planet ceased. For a moment nothing happened.

And then the earth shook.

At the indoctrination camp where Jeane had first met Urumqi, large green roots rose up and coiled themselves around the telescreens. It was the same elsewhere. In an explosion of sparks and shattered glass, they tore the screens down. Everywhere.

In military bases scattered across Kazaak, the ground trembled and soldiers ran terrified from their posts. They quivered in fear as the land reared up and folded in, crushing into dust endless rows of tanks with their steel treads.

In his hotel room, Xstersi gripped the couch to steady himself while tremors washed across the planet in great, cleansing waves. Staring out the window, he gasped in awe as massive roots wrapped around and entangled the high towers, but then lay still. There was no need for further destruction. It was plain for all to see.

Big Didi's rule was over.

-15-

Jeane left Wort on the immobilizer and after a short search found Urumqi's cell. The Arazi'ath was jubilant when she saw what had happened. It didn't take long for Xstersi to join them.

"Well, I guess that leaves you in charge," Jeane told Urumqi. "I trust you'll run things more fairly than your predecessor."

"What of Big Didi?" Urumqi asked.

"He's probably still on that table if he hasn't figured out I never did turn on the immobilizer," Jeane grinned.

"About the kvass," Xstersi hastily interjected, slithering forward, "I've a deal to—*urk!*"

Jeane pinched one of his tentacles. "I don't think now's the time, Xstersi. Urumqi has a lot to look after. Maybe later." She dragged the protesting Greelon away.

Jeane found a can of kvass in the customs station while they waited for the Transport Service vessel they'd called to pick them up. Leaning back, she tipped it to Xstersi. "Cheers!"

She popped it open and sipped the cool, refreshing drink.

Xstersi eyed the beer warily. "You know, Jeane, not telling me how kvass affects Greelons was a pretty dirty trick. Not something I'd expect from you."

"What're you talking about?" Jeane turned to him. "The kvass from the factory has no effect."

"But—"

"Whatever you felt," she smiled, "was all in your head."

-fin-

CRYOVACKED

...Unbelievably, sous vide cooking was first discovered by a human, Count Rumford, in 1799. This unique method of food preparation requires a pressurized enclosure within a partial or total vacuum. The good Count stumbled upon this insight when he accidentally left a roast mutton overnight in an experimental device, upon which he exclaimed, 'this is not merely eatable, but perfectly done, and most singularly well-tasted!' Much later, it was the Odysseus of our Order, Chef Hunter Jeane Oberon, who heralded it among the stars, though nearly at the cost of her life...

Excerpt from the Galactic Culinary Society's
Milky Way Review, Vol IV edition 3, N°314

-1-

His dreams were troubled.

Again.

Sir Benjamin Thompson, better known as Count Rumford, stood rumpled and disheveled in the yard of his ill-kept home in the sixteenth arrondissement of Paris. In the distance, the church bells of Notre-Dame d'Auteuil were chiming midnight. It was the twenty-first of August, 1814.

Unable to sleep, he busied himself turning a pulley, raising a small block of ice from the deep well where he'd stored it in winter.

But he couldn't escape his lingering visions.

My wife and daughter, he thought. *Has it been forty years since I left Massachusetts? My God, I'm already sixty-one. Why won't they let me rest! I didn't intend to abandon them!*

He laid a hand over his eyes. *It's best to think of my work. That's what's important. My experiment… I'm on the right track this time. I know it!* He turned his attention to the ice glinting in the moonlight. It dangled just below the lip of the well in a wooden bucket.

"The ice must emit invisible beams... *Frigorific rays*! I'm certain of it. How else can liquid solidify and freeze?"

While Rumford contemplated his misguided theory, a mysterious fog curiously began to gather, not far away, near the River Seine. Bubbles roiled up from deep beneath the surface of the black water.

Then, in a spray of foam, a shadowy form emerged. It floated to shore—concealed in the eerie mists—and stealthily crawled over the muddy riverbank.

Back at 59 rue d'Auteuil, Rumford's restive thoughts turned to another favorite gripe: *The rebel leader! Yes, he lived just around the corner from here during his stay in Paris,* Rumford recalled. *More famous and, dare I say it, admired for his scientific achievements... That damnable Franklin! But didn't I, Rumford, invent the drip coffee pot and the Rumford fireplace? What did Ben accomplish? Electricity? Revolution? Bah!*

At that very moment, tentacles were slithering through the fog over the damp cobblestones near the well-known Parisian inn, the Mouton Blanc, prudently staying out of the dim halo thrown by its swaying lanterns.

Rumford, meantime, mounted the steep steps to the attic workshop where his scientific apparatus was laid out. He placed the ice block on a metal tray.

He was reaching for his liquid-in-glass

thermometer when he heard a crash in the alley.

"Damn drunkards." He shook his head. He lined up his scale when the gate to his yard banged, followed by agitated hushing noises.

He went to the window. Over the dusky rooftops he made out the dim glow from the Mouton Blanc. Below, thick fog lay across the ground with tendrils corkscrewing from the open gate, into his yard.

"Hey! You can't go to the loo here!" he shouted. Then he added in French, as an afterthought, "Allez-vous en!"

He listened. Only silence. Did he see movement in the fog?

"Just an animal, I suppose." He went back to his metal tray but turned at the sound of dishes being knocked over in the kitchen below.

He grabbed a candle and went to the top of the stair. A note of alarm entered his voice. "Who's there?" He strained his hearing. It sounded like… Like something wet and unctuous being dragged over the floor. The noise one would expect a nest of snakes to make.

"Hello?" He gulped, feeling panic rising in his gut.

Something was at the bottom of the stair. Some looming, tentacled shadow which the light of his candle couldn't penetrate. Then it separated and broke into smaller, slithering shapes.

Rumford backed away terror stricken. "Help! Demons! Help! Someone!"

At his cry, the shapes scurried up. One of the creatures stopped and looked at him, its face covered by a strange clear mask filled with gurgling liquid topped by two waggling eyestalks.

The Greelon turned and ordered his fellows, "Better bag him. Quick!"

-2-

A couple of centuries later, a Greelon ferry-pod carried another group of passengers through the vast loneliness of space to their destination near a gas-giant englobed with swirling, orange-coloured clouds.

"I hope you appreciate the enormity of this, Jeane."

"Oh, I don't doubt our expedition cost you a pretty penny, Xstersi." Jeane Oberon adjusted her oxygen mask to look at the Greelon floating in a clear blue liquid—which filled the entire vessel. Normally in an oxygen type atmosphere he needed to wear a water-mask, but not here. In this Greelon ship it was Jeane—being human—who required a wetsuit.

Xstersi cocked his eyestalks at her. "Why don't you ever trust me?"

"Something to do with past experience." She pushed herself from her seat and swam through the liquid to get a better view out the cockpit window.

"But truly, this time it has nothing to do with *me*. My businesses have nothing to gain. It's my son who invited us! Well, he invited me. Needless to say, I've been bankrolling his venture, but when he told me about his latest discovery… I knew I had to ask you along, especially after how you helped me out with that little problem on Slurtia Six!"

"As I recall, we nearly died on Slurtia Six."

"Have some faith! Very soon, you're going to witness—yes, even taste—something extraordinary, and you'll get to bring all the details back to your precious Galactic Culinary Society. Once again, Jeane Oberon will be declared the greatest Chef Hunter in all the universe!"

"I can hardly wait," she answered dryly.

"Come look, you can see it now." Another Greelon swam back from the ship's controls to point with a grey tentacle.

Xstersi blithely shoved him aside. "Thank you, Xasterstosopophane."

Jeane turned to the second Greelon. She could never get a handle on their long, unpronounceable names; Xstersi was the shortened form of *Xstersiisterpeeze*. "You're the Director of Antiquities on Greelon, aren't you?"

The Director nodded excitedly. "Xstersi's son made the discovery of the century! That ship you see there disappeared over a hundred and twenty years ago: the lost Emperor's Flagship!"

Jeane squinted and saw a long, black shape outlined against the bright planet. At first, it appeared as no more than a tiny spec, but soon it filled their view. She estimated it to be more than a kilometer in length, armored in plate corals piled one atop the other. Massive coral pillars stood up at what she guessed to be the tail-end, like fins.

"Like a coral reef floating in space," she mused.

"We don't make them like that anymore," The Director of Antiquities, Xaster, cogitated. "A fine example, the finest, from the Late Greelon Imperial period."

"Humph. Now, all our ships come from the Skylar," Xstersi groused, though he too was awed by the monstrous ship dwarfing their tiny ferry-pod. His eyestalks followed the length of the dark, desolate looking vessel.

"It looks completely dead inside," Jeane said in the hushed silence.

"Xstersi's son has been slowly powering it up."

Sure enough, as they came around the stern, a yellow light gleamed from under tall coral pillars: the docking port. More dim lights were visible along the underside. Through these portholes, Jeane saw a greenish-blue liquid sloshing around, much like in their ferry-pod.

"Good thing I dressed appropriately." She double checked her oxygen supply on her wrist computer and slung an extra canister over her shoulder.

The Director of Antiquities brought them face-to-face with the docking port with a few spurts of their directional thrusters.

There was a dull clang and the ships locked together. Jeane heard the gurgling of methane water filling the exchange chamber. Xaster, the Director of Antiquities, pulled a lever and the water-lock hissed open. A greenish-blue liquid swirled in, mixing with the sky-blue water of their ferry-pod. The liquid carried with it the smell of aged, fermented sugar which penetrated her breathing mask. Jeane wrinkled her nose.

"After you." The Director of Antiquities waved a tentacle invitingly.

-3-

Xstersi swam into the dark ship, his oculars glancing from side to side. "Come along, Jeane! I want to introduce you to my number one son!"

Jeane followed, wondering if she shouldn't have brought along a pair of swim-flippers. It was a big ship.

She noted the interior was made of the same rough looking corals as the exterior. The sensation was like entering an underwater cave or tunnel. With little sense of up or down, she reminded herself to keep an eye on her bearings. She swam close to one wall and stretched out a gloved hand to gently touch a faintly glowing, gel-like filament.

"The ship's old power system," Xaster explained, noticing her curiosity. "It wasn't easy for us to master electricity as an underwater species, but those are gel-tubes filled with an ionized solution which is highly conductive. They run throughout the ship. Today, we use modern systems which we get from the Ummotti."

"Enough with the put-me-to-sleep history lesson! Where's Wextersissopixes?" Xstersi interjected. "Ah, there's my boy!"

A bright light came swiftly around the bend, carried by a hurriedly swimming Greelon. At first glance, Jeane couldn't tell them apart. But then she saw this one had a smoother, less wrinkled epidermis and was obviously younger.

"Pops, you made it!" The young Greelon beamed.

"Jeane, I'd like you to meet my number one son. You can call him Wexter. The best of my brood! He was even the first to be hatched, would you believe it? The things he's achieved! Did you know, he established the first Greelon off-planet university? It was just a copy of the Brain Coral back home, but Greelons flocked to it anyway! Such dupes! To save money, he never gave out degrees—he just flunked everyone! That only made them more interested— the prestige of such a hard to pass program! And he was the one who ran the marketing campaign for Kvass: The Best Beer in the Universe, sure to get you smashed without a hangover! To be fair, you couldn't get so much as lightheaded from it, and the cheaply produced formula tasted like piss—but we raked it in! What have the other hundred and forty-seven useless, sad-sack Greelings constantly mooching off me ever accomplished?! And now look what he's found!"

"I didn't realize you had such a big family," Jeane said, shaking her head at the thought of all those little Xstersis running amok in the cosmos.

"Worthless! Every last one of them!"

"Alright, dad. I wouldn't have been able to do it without your help. Now, don't you want to see what you came here for?"

"Right, right lad. Lead the way!"

As they swam down the corridor, Jeane couldn't help noticing how the young Greelon looked funnily at his father, but Xstersi didn't seem to catch it.

"How far is it to the kitchen, Wexter-my-boy?"

"Right now we're in the stern. The Imperial Kitchens are near the bow, just below the bridge."

"We've an amazing surprise in store for you, Jeane, if everything Wexter here has told me is true!"

"I've been waiting with bated breath. Though you could've told me before what it is—"

"Where would the fun be in that? Trust me!"

"Uh-huh." Jeane shook her head. She'd known Xstersi long enough not to pry any further. She would just have to wait and see. She touched the Universal-Translator-Tab behind her helmet, turning off the signal which sent simultaneous translations through her cochlea. She listened to the barks, honks, and clicks of the Greelons, so obviously more efficient for communicating underwater than human speech. She switched the Trans-Tab back on.

Jeane addressed Xaster, the Director of Antiquities, swimming on her right side. He politely slowed while Xstersi and his son —Greelons being proficient swimmers—bobbed ahead. "My understanding is that the Last Greelon Emperor escaped the Revolution in this ship?"

"That's right," Xaster answered. "Shadaxaxtissisiesy the XXXVIth, last of the Bull-Emperors, didn't agree with turning Greelon into a Republic—like it is today. He dreamed of returning to a Greelon Golden Age, holding on to power until the bitter end. When he saw the tide was going against him, he fled—in this ship—through an unmarked wormhole off the main Astrolink. He and his most loyal supporters were never seen again."

"How did Wexter find his ship?"

"He said he came across old, encrypted transmissions, and was able to break the code. It led him here."

As they talked, Jeane saw they had entered a large, cavernous hall with stalactite-like protrusions hanging from the dark ceiling while even more stalagmites rose up from the floor in twisting profusion. They swam between them.

"The Imperial Library," Xaster explained.

"What became of the crew?" Jeane asked.

"We've been respectfully cleaning up."

"Everyone aboard died?"

"Yes... Apparently, violently."

-4-

Perceiving that the bright, weaving light of Wexter and Xstersi had moved further ahead, leaving them in only the dim ruddiness of Jeane's helmet, Xaster hurried their pace to catch up.

They passed under a wide arch and Jeane caught her breath. They'd entered an immense, cavernous room. *Hard to believe we're still in a ship*, she thought.

"Look here!" Wexter called. He waved his light, catching the gleam of tall stalagmites in the center of the chamber. As he passed his beam over them, Jeane noticed the stalagmites were spaced out in a rough semi-circle. Delicately carved Greelon lettering ran up and down them in gold. The space in the middle of the formation was lost in inky blackness.

Jeane swam up to them.

"And here's," Wexter breathed, "The Emperor himself."

He shined his light into the strange structure. The glittering beam picked out a hulking, skeletal form with desiccated, leathery skin clinging here and there. Wexter's light traced a long tentacle, twice Jeane's height, floating in the stagnant fluid. In the wavering shadows it was hard to tell, but she guessed the creature to be as large as a city bus. A far cry from the Greelons she'd encountered, most of whom were no more than three or four feet tall.

"The Last Bull-Emperor," Xaster said. "We're in the throne room."

"That's one humongous son-of-a-gun," Xstersi murmured enviously.

"There was only one Bull-Emperor at a time," The Director of Antiquities explained. "Generally speaking, a single *Bull Male* heir would hatch among his Greelings. Even then, the Emperor wouldn't give up power willingly. Inevitably, the son had to overthrow his father." He cast an eye on the eerie remains. "But not this time."

"Rough." Xstersi shook his head. Again, Jeane caught the curious, fleeting glare Wexter cast at his father. What was he thinking, she wondered?

"Shall we continue to the kitchens?" the Director of Antiquities asked in the lull. "That's why you requested Jeane's presence, isn't it? To assist with our little problem."

Jeane turned to Xstersi. She should have expected something like this. "What little problem?"

He coughed sheepishly. "It's nothing much."

"Oh, really?"

"He's right," Wexter intervened. "The Emperor has, well *had*," he glanced at the hulking cadaver, "a human machine which we thought you could help operate."

"I thought you invited me for *a surprise*?" Jeane stared intently at Xstersi.

"Heh. Surprise." He shrugged his tentacles.

"I suppose you thought you'd have to pay for my expertise? Or at least make a donation to the Culinary Society?"

Xstersi turned his eyestalks away guiltily.

"Alright. Anyway, I'm here. How is it that the Greelons have a human device? This ship disappeared before Initial Contact."

"The Emperor went on a Grand Galactic Tour," Xaster answered. "His servants picked up anything they thought might interest or entertain him."

"In this case they selected a human male from your planet," Wexter added.

"You mean, *abducted*?"

The three Greelons nodded.

"Go on." Jean sighed.

"His name was Benjamin Thomson, count of Rumford. A scientist."

"Rumford? I've heard of him. He died in Paris, in 1814. Greelons weren't supposed to be on Earth, by the way."

The three Greelons didn't appear troubled by this breach of Galactic Law. Well, it *was* in the past, Jeane thought.

"Extraction teams left behind a look-a-like corpse," Xaster clarified. "Subjects were never returned."

"This Rumford made a device—like no other—which prepared the Emperor's favorite dish. A rare delicacy. The very last one is onboard. We thought you might be able to decipher the human controls," Wexter concluded.

"What became of Rumford?"

"Considering your short human lifespan, he probably died on Greelon before the Emperor fled. The records from those chaotic times are a mess."

"It's just like we said," Xstersi impatiently interrupted. "My number one son has made the find of the century. The last Imperial Quibble Eggs are on this ship!"

-5-

Jeane saw Wexter could no longer hold in whatever was bothering him.

"Dad, there's something I need to tell you —"

But Xstersi cut him off. "Enough with the chit-chatting. Why are we still hanging around this old bag of bones? Lead the way, Wexter!"

"But dad, you need to know—"

"Nothing's so important it can't wait until our bellies are full with our Imperial repast, number one!"

"Dad, I'm not your number one!"

Jeane and Xaster looked at Wexter inquiringly. Xstersi stared blankly. "What?"

"I'm... I'm actually the one-hundred and forty-ninth... entirely ignored... and completely forgotten of your children."

"What's this nonsense? I only have a hundred-and-forty-eight Greelings!"

"I was the last to hatch."

"Last to—?"

"You didn't wait around."

"Who has the time to watch a hundred-and-forty-eight Greelings hatch?!"

"One-hundred-and-forty-*nine*."

Xstersi furrowed his eyestalks, his expression darkening. "Is this some kind of scam?"

"I can assure your paternity, dad. Not that you ever paid attention to any of us. You can't even tell the real Wextersissopixes and me apart. Shows how much you care!"

"I guess you want moolah off me? Benefits? An allowance?"

"Dad, I—"

"Well, you can forget it! And don't call me dad! Now, whoever you are — take us to the kitchen so we can get this farce over with!" Xstersi waved a tentacle angrily.

"My name is Yanxyiopiocasixes." Yanxy narrowed his eyestalks darkly. "Wait here. I have to turn on the kitchen's power first." Yanxy swam off irritably. Presently, his light disappeared around a corner.

"Why are you so upset?" Jeane turned to Xstersi. "He seemed genuine. Do you think he's a fraud?"

Xstersi scrunched his whole body into an indignant ball — and squirted out a little puff of black ink. "No. He's probably who he says he is. It wouldn't be hard for the Brain Coral to prove, after all."

"Then what is it?"

"He lied to me! Me and my brood might swindle our way across the galaxy, but we never, ever con each other! He's a no-good, back-stabbing, double-crossing—"

"You mean, he got the better of you?"

Xstersi sighed. "Don't try to talk me out of my righteous anger, Jeane. I'm the wronged party here!"

Just then a loud, mechanical clang reverberated throughout the chamber, cutting short their discussion.

"What was that?" Xstersi's eyestalks scanned the dark water.

The Director of Antiquities looked around worriedly. "I didn't like the sound of it, whatever it was."

Through her helmet lights, Jeane noticed the room's fluid had started to flow in a single direction. Previously it had been stagnant.

"I think we'd better—"

Another clang shook the chamber. Suddenly, the water turned into churning, torrential rapids, sucking them to—

"The water-lock's opened — Ahhh!" Xaster, the Director of Antiquities, screeched as the current flushed him into the vacuum of space.

Jeane braced herself against the stalagmites surrounding the remains of the Greelon Emperor. She glanced up and saw an oval water-lock had opened above them.

Xstersi meanwhile, was flapping his tentacles with all his might, swimming against the current gushing into space. But he couldn't keep it up.

With the water raging around her, Jeane peered

up at the opening. There, those red markings had to be—?

She let go of the stalagmite and straightened her body, like an arrow.

She shot past Xstersi, up, towards the opening. But she was going too fast! She wasn't going to make it. No, she could just reach it. She stretched out and grabbed the bar next to the red lettering and pulled hard.

The water-lock ground to a close even as Xstersi flopped against it, dragged there by the last of the escaping water.

Jeane breathed a sigh of relief. Then she saw they weren't out of danger yet. With the chamber empty of water, Xstersi floated in zero-gravity. His tentacles grabbed frantically at his throat-sac. Of course, he couldn't breathe!

Jeane looked around the water-lock. Yes, there! She scrambled around, picked out an emergency water-mask and pushed off.

She slammed into Xstersi and quickly fitted the water-mask over his head. It was an old one; would it still work? She opened the valve on the attached tank. Greenish-brown liquid flowed into Xstersi's mask.

"Bah! That stinks!"

"At least you're still alive. The Director of Antiquities wasn't so lucky."

"What happened?"

"The water-lock opened."

"No kidding, Jeane. But how?"

She thought carefully, gathering her breath. "It could have been an accident. But it seems unlikely. Who else is on this ship?"

"Just us! I arranged to have everyone sent away so I—we—could enjoy the Quibble Eggs to ourselves."

"Very forward thinking of you."

Xstersi furrowed his eyestalks in contemplation. "Of course, Wexter, or whatever his name is, very conveniently disappeared just before."

"Yanxy," Jeane reminded him of his son's true name. Could he have been behind it?

"Yes, yes! That's it!" Xstersi's eyestalks lit up with a malicious light. "Don't you see, Jeane? It was a set up! A ruse to lure me here. Unfortunately for you, I dragged you along. Sorry I got you mixed up in all this... Well, not really. Better than dying alone."

Jeane shrugged her shoulders. "What was the point?"

"It's obvious, isn't it? He already had the Director of Antiquities thinking he was my number one son, Wextersissopixes. How many others did he fool? Must've *offed* poor Wexter... Fratricide has a long Greelon history, you can imagine."

"With so many siblings..."

"—My business empire will fall to him."

"Won't the Brain Coral prove...?"

"Why would anyone check? No, this Yanxy has

everything tied up nicely."

"I don't suppose you did like King Lear and divided up—?"

"King who—?"

"Never mind."

"All my holdings go to Wexter."

"You didn't leave anything for the others?"

"A small stipend. You don't know what it's like being a Greelon, Jeane. Wexter was the only one I could trust."

"Maybe it's time to reevaluate that philosophy?"

"Could we please stop discussing my *Last Will and Testament*. We're still alive, aren't we? How are *you* going to get us out of here?"

"I'll see what I can do." Jeane assumed she could remember the way back to the ferry-pod. She'd paid close attention to their route.

She glanced across the long chamber. The entrance had automatically sealed to prevent more methane water from escaping. She was floating in zero-gravity. How to get across?

Jeane let out a touch of air from her extra oxygen-supply canister. It propelled her toward the door. *Hate having to waste it*, she thought.

Xstersi, like all Greelons, was more adept in a zero-G environment. With one of his tentacles, he found a piece of floating debris left by the deluge and gently pushed off, following her.

"Yanxy probably believes we're dead. Still, we have to be careful with him out there," he said.

"Do you think he'll go straight to the ferry-pod?"

Jeane tried the door seal while Xstersi considered her question. "It's no good. It's locked. We're stuck," she said.

Xstersi wasn't listening. "The Imperial Quibble Eggs… Jeane, while we're here, we have to get those eggs!"

She looked at him. Was it worth the risk?

"Yanxy assumes we're dead, right? Where do you think he's going? We can get the drop on him, and the eggs!"

"Maybe he already smuggled them out?"

"He never had a chance before. Too many eyes aboard."

"We don't know where the kitchens are, remember? This ship's a maze."

"Can't you do *something*?"

Jeane deliberated. Yes, maybe… She activated her wrist computer. "A while back, I visited the Greelon Bureau of Records to get info on an old Trader named Hoargar—"

"You mean, you broke in."

"Anyway, with the time constraint, I made a large file dump. Let's see what there is…"

She rifled through her records while Xstersi anxiously watched.

"Here we go. Schematics for the Imperial Flagship."

"Then what are you waiting for? We have to beat Yanxy to the kitchen!"

"Didn't you hear when I said the door's locked?"

"When has that ever stopped you?"

"Alright, just give me a minute to think of a way."

"We don't have a minute. Yanxy has a head start!"

Jeane ignored him and examined the chamber. There had to be something useful.

Without water it was easier to see in the dim light provided by the faintly luminescent, ionized gel-tubes lining the walls.

"Can't we go out through the water-lock? It's manual. If you closed it, we can open it," Xstersi offered helpfully.

"And go across the hull? We don't have spacesuits. Even if we found a Greelon one, and I don't see any here, what are the odds of a human suit being aboard?" she answered, disregarding his impatiently fidgeting tentacles.

She wondered: in the past when the door seal was closed, how would *He* have gotten out?

In the center of the gloomy chamber the massive remains of the Bull-Emperor were lodged among the throne-like formation. Skeletal tentacles had randomly wrapped themselves around the stalagmites preventing his evacuation into space.

Surely the Greelon Emperor would never be locked in?

"Wait here." She pushed off. Xstersi kept an ocular on her as she floated across and caught hold of one of the stalagmites surrounding the Bull-Emperor.

She was attempting something but Xstersi couldn't tell what, only that she was tugging on one of the Emperor's long, emaciated tentacles.

After a moment, Jeane floated back.

"Let's see if this works." She held up a tentacle tip with a skeletal suction-cup on its end which she'd detached with her laser-knife. "Better stand aside. The corridor's still filled with methane water."

Jeane waved the bony suction-cup alongside the seal. It scanned the Emperor's *tentacle print.* Groaning, the door —shaped like the mouth of a starfish— opened.

Without the vacuum draining power of space this time, a giant globule of greenish-blue liquid slowly squeezed through.

"Better shake a tentacle, Jeane." Xstersi wrapped one of his own around her, pushing her into the liquid filled corridor. He grabbed the edge of the door seal and swung through after her.

They were just in time. The door snapped shut, cutting the amorphous blob of water in two. Like a balloon it floated aimlessly into the throne room.

In the now dark and empty chamber there was no one left to see the ponderous remains of the Greelon Emperor slowly begin to twitch…

-6-

Jeane and Xstersi raced through the long corridors of the ship. Xstersi was in a mighty hurry to get to the kitchens in time to cut off Yanxy, and Jeane had to push herself to her limits just to keep up with the fervid Greelon. Still, she was trailing behind.

Fortunately, at every junction he'd pause and call back, "which way, which way?" while she consulted the map displayed on her wrist computer.

Finally, he stopped in front of a scabrous looking door, reading the gold lettering above it.

"What will you do when you find Yanxy?" Jeane asked, catching her breath. "I hope you won't do anything you'll regret."

"Never mind that. Pass me the Emperor's tentacle piece. I think I've found a way to even the score."

Jeane handed the bony protuberance to him. "What is it?"

The door bubbled open.

"The Emperor's personal cabin."

They swam in.

In the far corner, Jeane saw what looked like

a giant open clam, pearly smooth. The Bull-Emperor's bed chamber?

Xstersi didn't pay any attention to it, instead swimming to a large console set with faintly glowing corals. Innumerable gel-tubes ran in and out of it.

"He could control the whole ship from here," Xstersi muttered. His eyestalks lit up keenly.

Jeane looked it over. "Without the Emperor's, uhm, passcode, no one's had access to this before."

Xstersi nodded in agreement. "When Yanxy booted up the ship, power must've been fed to this central console." A wicked sheen lit his face.

"Xstersi? What do you have in mind?"

He ignored her, tentacles flicking quickly over the board. The controls were unfamiliar to her so she couldn't follow what he was doing.

"Aha! I've found him. There!" He pointed. Jeane saw a dim, red light flashing on the console. "He's in the dining hall. He hasn't made it to the kitchen yet."

"What about this other, fainter light in the throne room?" she asked.

"That's nothing. Just a glitch. This is clearly the signature of a Greelon!"

"How can you be sure it's him?"

She didn't like where Xstersi appeared to be taking this. He looked half-crazed; consumed by anger.

The Greelon toggled another switch. "Yanxy, my vile, devious offspring, I want you to hear my voice. Can you hear me?"

There was a pause, then a voice crackled over the ship's speaker. It was Yanxy.

"Dad? What happened? When I went out, the door to the throne room sealed and—"

"Don't play the innocent with me! I know all about your scheme!"

"Scheme? Dad, what're you—?"

"Enough with this useless banter. Your time's up! *What's sauce for the goose*—"

Realizing what he was about to do, Jeane lunged. "Xstersi, no!"

But she was too late. Xstersi slammed the button. The force of his thrust shorted out the ancient console even as the sound of gushing water filled the speakers.

"Flushed into space, like he intended for us! Good riddance!" Xstersi spat at the defunct control board.

"You didn't have to do that!" Jeane admonished him.

"He tried to kill us! And he would have kept on trying!"

"You don't know—"

"Don't impose your human values on me, Jeane! And don't pretend you know what Greelons are really like. You don't know anything about my family! Now, let's get to the kitchen, get the damn Quibble Eggs, and get out of here!"

Jeane stared hard at him. To her mind he had gone too far this time. "I have the map. How're you going to get there without my help?"

They were at an impasse.

Finally, Xstersi growled. "Really, Jeane? I know *you* too well. Are you going to pass up this chance?"

At length, Jeane sighed.

He was right.

-7-

Both in a somber mood now, Jeane and Xstersi swam through the winding corridors toward the Imperial Kitchens. Jeane noted she only had two hours left of air but figured it should be enough considering they'd be heading home soon.

"Looks like the Director of Antiquities never got around to cleaning up here," Xstersi muttered as they swam into a series of low-ceilinged warrens.

Scattered Greelon corpses floated throughout the dark chamber.

"This is it," Jeane said. "The Imperial Kitchen." She shined her helmet light on a skeleton. "Laser burns. Xaster was right. They killed each other. I wonder what set them off?"

"It doesn't matter. Just look for the human machine. It shouldn't be hard for you to spot. I'll find the Quibble Eggs," he grumbled.

Jeane glanced at him. What was going on in his three brains? Regret? *Too late for that now,* she thought. *Better find what we came here for and get out.*

They swam in opposite directions through severed bits of tentacle.

Jeane ducked into an alcove full of strange Greelon machinery. A green, semi-luminescent rock was visible in a thick, oven-like window. Radioactive Autunite. Tubes ran from it to various cooking devices throughout the chamber.

In another alcove, she observed what appeared to be alien (at least, non-Greelon) equipment. This looks more promising, she reflected. Obviously, the late Bull-Emperor had exotic tastes.

She was searching the room when a familiar, metallic gleam caught her eye. There—? She swam over.

Yes. Stainless steel! The shiny, human-made material stood out like a sore thumb among all the grey corals. Jeane swam right up to it, thoughtlessly pushing a decrepit corpse aside in her excitement. No doubt finding something *human* among all this alienness touched her, pushing Yanxy's death out of her mind.

A small metal box was mounted on a coral protrusion. A handle—with a human fitted grip —poked out of it, next to a dial. A black power-cable ran out the back encased in a gluey, yellow substance, presumably added to waterproof it. Plainly stamped on the front in the Latin-Anglo alphabet was: *Troisgros*.

"I've found it!" Jeane called.

"And I've found the Quibble Egg! There was only one left in the carton. It really is the last one!"

Xstersi swam over holding up a dull, spotted egg. She could easily enclose her hand around it. So small?

Each eyeing what the other had found, they exclaimed in unison, "That's it?"

"When it's especially prepared, you won't believe what this tastes like!" Xstersi declared. "Or at least, so they say."

Jeane indicated the stainless steel box. "This is a *sous-vide* device."

"Sue-veed?"

"From a human dialect, meaning *in-vacuum*."

"I don't get it..."

"As in, cooked in a vacuum. First, you have to put your ingredients in a vacuum-sealed container or plastic-wrap. Then you place it in this box, which is filled with water and heated to a precise temperature by a circulator. We call it, *cryovacking*."

"What's the point of going through all that?" Xstersi eyed the sous-vide machine suspiciously.

"Think of it. If you're roasting or grilling—or heating with Autunite, as Greelons do—you need high levels of heat, and you can easily overcook. It's not very accurate. You never really know what's happening *inside*. On the other hand, if you *could* cook at a lower temperature... it results in much higher succulence. That's what can be achieved with sous-vide." Jeane noticed Xstersi had started to drool. She continued. "The cell-walls in plant-based foods remain intact yet softened. With meats, collagen is hydrolyzed into gelatin, which is good, while the protein doesn't get too tough or lose its moisture. All because the food can't get any hotter than the water-bath it's in. Of course, it's often necessary to cook for very long times: twenty-four, even forty-eight hours. But it's impossible to overcook with sous-vide. All the flavors are increased and retained in the vacuum-sealed bag."

"What about this?" Xstersi held up the Quibble Egg.

"Its own shell is the vacuum-seal. You can place it directly in the sous-vide device."

"Good, good."

"Also, eggs develop a texture in sous-vide you can't get any other way: the whites become soft and *satiny* while the yolk turns jelly-like."

She saw Xstersi was practically slavering now.

"The final benefit," she added, "is that because of the precise nature of sous-vide, the results are always the same. You have complete control."

"Oh, the Emperor would have loved that, I bet. He was known to execute servants for an improperly cooked meal."

"Yes, this little machine probably saved a few heads," Jeane agreed.

"Put it in, put it in!" Xstersi urged.

"What? Weren't you paying attention? I said it takes time, and I don't have much air." She glanced at the sous-vide device. "It's overgrown by coral. We can't remove it without damaging it. But don't worry, I can replicate it. It's not complicated."

"But I want my Quibble Egg cooked in the

Emperor's own machine!" Xstersi pleaded.

Jeane saw he was getting that fervent light in his oculars again. Out of curiosity, she pressed the dial on the sous-vide device. It lit up.

"Looks like you're in luck. Assuming these last settings were for the Quibble Egg, it'll only take thirty-five minutes." She glanced at her chronometer. Should be enough time, she decided, even leaving them some room to maneuver in case anything came up. "You can put it in."

Xstersi opened the lid and reverently popped in the Quibble Egg. "Your Count Rumford certainly invented a marvelous machine!"

"Rumford couldn't have made this." Jeane shook her head. "He discovered sous-vide by accident when he left a shoulder of mutton overnight in an experimental convention oven, and his servants found it the next day. He never called it sous-vide, and he was using eighteenth century technology. He just discovered the benefits of low-temperature cooking." She examined the stainless steel box more closely. "No, this looks like a Pralus-device from the nineteen-seventies, in Earth years. It was made by a French chef at a restaurant called *Troisgros*. I wonder how it got here?"

"Just turn it on!"

"It's on," she said. "We have to wait."

Xstersi swam in an excited little twirl. "Oh, I can't wait... I can't wait!" He clapped his tentacles enthusiastically.

While they both patiently watched the

humming sous-vide box, neither noticed that from out of two tubular corals behind them, a large, plastic-like substance was slowly being secreted.

-8-

"What's that?!" Xstersi exclaimed. A clear, filmy substance clung to his tentacles like a spider's web. The thin plastic sheeting had wrapped around Jeane's legs too. She reflexively swam up, away from it, but that only made it worse, pulling the substance more quickly out of the emission tube. It folded over her head, blindly knocking away her extra oxygen canister.

She reached for the laser-cutter on her belt, but too late. The plastic wrapping enveloped her hand. She couldn't grip the laser. In seconds, she was completely sealed in.

Jeane floated motionless swathed in a transparent plastic cocoon. Straining her eyes, she glanced at the chronometer on her immobilized wrist. Ten minutes of oxygen!

Out of the corner of her vision, she saw Xstersi flailing in the plastic wrap. With his many tentacles he madly tried to shrug it off. No, he was failing. His exertions subsided.

Had they accidentally activated this food sealant? Jeane wondered. Or... Yanxy? Had he—? No way to communicate through the plastic seal.

And something else. Jeane felt dizzy, beginning to sweat. The temperature was rising.

In the adjacent alcove the Autunite pulsed with a deadly glow.

The ship's speakers crackled to life.

"Well, well. I finally have the assassins! The traitors!" That voice. It was human. But what was he talking about? Traitors?

In the Imperial Throne Room, a shadowy figure stirred *within* the embrace of the skeletal tentacles of the late Bull-Emperor, concealed there by leathery folds of decaying skin. A wispy-haired old man in a bubble-helmet peered out.

One hand, deeply wrinkled and liver spotted, gripped the stalagmite where he had bolted the Emperor to it. The other hand held up a control-pad — but it was no hand at all! A Greelon tentacle had been grafted onto the wrist!

He spoke into the control-pad. "Once before you attempted to assassinate *Mon Seigneur*. But you failed then, just as you've failed now! Sneaking aboard... pretending to be loyalists during our long exile... bearing gifts from Earth... The very same machine you see before you. Only, this time I've used it against you!"

Who could it be, Jeane wondered? *Mon Seigneur*. French, for *My Lord*. It couldn't be—? That was too long ago. She had to get out of the plastic seal. It was getting too hot, and she couldn't think straight. If he'd just shut up... Maybe she could...

"His Excellency will be so pleased with me. Just

like when King George the Third knighted me for betraying the dastardly American rebels. Charged *me* with being unfriendly to the cause of liberty?! Bah! I've never been disloyal in my life! Yes, I left my wife and daughter, but what choice did I have? A mob attacked our house! Better to die with fealty in my heart than a turncoat!"

Jeane remembered. Rumford, born in Massachusetts, sided with Britain during the War of Independence. He fled to England and was richly rewarded.

"And what about you, traitors? Are my *calorific* rays getting to you? Feeling a little hot under the collar, eh? No? Perhaps you desire a pair of my patented thermal underwear? Oh, ho! I invented that too! Mon Seigneur prized my great intellect. How I regaled him with my stories. I even served him *Rumford's soup.* I invented *that* to help the poor. To be sure, his Excellency didn't enjoy it so much, so he... Never mind! When the Republicans pulled out their disintegrators—"

What was he blabbering about now? Events on Earth, or Greelons? Everything was a haze. It wasn't just the heat, Jeane realized. Oxygen depletion. One minute left.

"—I Cryovacked myself at subzero temperatures. Like they'd done to me so many times before, whenever his Lordship got in one of his moods... The nightmare sleep! Yes, I did it when the so-called Loyalists —who'd snuck aboard — began their attack. Not because I was a coward, no! But because I knew… I *knew* it was the best way to preserve myself to better serve his Excellency! Then, the little demons unwittingly thawed me out when they powered up the ship. And now… Now it's your turn. Except, at a hundred-and-forty-five degrees, you'll be precisely cooked over the next five hundred years—in the vacuum of space!"

Rumford broke off in a mad chortle.

Through drooping eyelids, Jeane saw Xstersi had begun to flail again. His plastic cocoon whirled and thrashed, spinning wildly.

His death throes. Jeane wouldn't have thought it, but she was sad to see him go this way. She knew she wasn't far behind. No, she couldn't give up. But what?

As her consciousness faded, Jeane saw Xstersi break through the plastic seal. With his free tentacle he slashed all along the cocoon, slicing it open. How could—?

Xstersi darted over to Jeane and hurriedly went to work, cutting her free.

"Jeane, Jeane!" He shook her, but she didn't respond. "Too late!"

He spotted the extra air canister floating nearby. He quickly reattached it. "Jeane?"

Sweat dripping down her forehead, she tiredly opened her eyes and inhaled a deep breath. "Xstersi? How?"

"We're even now, Jeane, for all those times you saved me." He held up the sharp, bony tentacle tip from the Greelon Emperor. "I had it the whole time and nearly forgot!"

"The advantage of having many appendages." Jeane grinned.

Xstersi swam to the door, but it slid shut as soon as he reached it. He waved the Emperor's suction cup in front of the seal.

"Jeane, the code's been changed!"

Rumford's voice hissed over the ship's speakers. "So, you escaped my sous-vide trap? It doesn't matter. You'll just be overcooked. I'm increasing the temperature!"

The Autunite's glow intensified.

Jeane shook the fogginess from her mind. *Out of the frying pan and into the fire* — if ever a saying applied to their situation. What to do?

Xstersi swum glumly over.

"Sorry, Jeane. I thought I had it. In the plastic there was a little bubble of methane to breathe... But this heat is worse on me."

Jeane nodded. There had to be something they could do. She'd nearly given up before. She wasn't about to again.

"What about poor Yanxy, Jeane? It wasn't his fault!"

"We'll commiserate later, Xstersi. Try to focus on the problem at hand." She examined the door. If she plugged in her wrist computer? No, this was the Imperial Flagship. It would take time to break the encryption, time they didn't have. She felt the heat dangerously rising.

Xstersi continued to mope. "Why did I do it? Why didn't I listen when I had the chance? Yanxy, wherever you are, your pop's sorry. Anyway, I'll be joining you soon!"

Jeane considered. Maybe she was looking at their situation the wrong way. They needed time. So how to gain time? Reduce the temperature. Would that be easier? She glanced around the room. The pulsing Autunite. The sous-vide machine.

Maybe?

"Rumford! We're not after your Emperor. We just want to get off this ship," she called out.

"A likely story. Ha! Why should I trust you? I must protect the Emperor!"

"Open your eyes! He's already dead!" Xstersi blurted.

"What?! What're you talking about? Are you mad?"

"Oh, sheesh." The Greelon shook his head. "There's no arguing with this nut-ball."

With Rumford distracted, Jeane swam closer to the stainless steel box, countering, "but I'm also human, like you."

For a moment, the speakers were silent. At last, they heard, "Yes... Oh, yes. It's been so long... The sound of a human voice. A woman's voice! You remind me of... No, you're trying to trick me." Then more angrily, "You're a traitor!"

Jeane had already set to work while they were talking. She traced back an ionized gel-tube from the Autunite to a junction near the sous-vide machine. She carefully detached the tube, then pulled out the black, human made wire from the Pralus-device. She had to be careful. It was so hot. Perspiration clouded her vision. Her hands were slick with sweat inside her gloves. *If it shorts out...* She plugged in the glowing gel-tube.

"Yes! Any electrical current can carry a signal," Xstersi whispered.

She dialed back the Pralus-device.

Would it work?

"The Autunite's fading!" Xstersi declared.

"No. You can't do that!" Rumford yelled over the speakers. "Override!" In the throne room, he frantically thumbed the control-pad.

"We're still stuck in here." Xstersi turned to Jeane, breathing a sigh of relief as the temperature dropped. "It won't be long before he gets it working again."

"At least we have a chance now." She'd bought them extra time. Would it be enough? Have to keep Rumford off his game, she thought. What had he said? She searched her memory. He'd mentioned...

"Rumford," Jeane called tentatively. "What would your wife and daughter think if they saw you now? Your... *Sarah.*"

In response, there was only a static hiss from the speakers. Then they nearly exploded. "Don't mention that name!" Rumford furiously pounded the control-pad.

"Jeane, we gotta get out of here!" Xstersi

implored. They looked around helplessly—when in a shower of sparks the door suddenly burst open, and Yanxy swam in carrying a disintegrator pistol.

"Pops!" The young Greelon swam over and embraced his father. "You're safe!"

"Yanxy! Alive and come to your old man's rescue. Thank the Gods of Greelon!"

"When I heard you say you're sorry over the ship's speakers, I headed straight over. Though to be frank, I thought about abandoning you at first."

"You're here now!"

"How did you do it?" Jeane asked.

"Luck, I guess. I was to one side of the water-lock when it opened — and was able to get a tentacle around the emergency handle. Most of the methane water escaped, but there was a bubble large enough to encompass me. It wasn't easy to maneuver it to the door."

"How did you get out?"

Yanxy held up the disintegrator gun. "From the final battle between Loyalists and Republicans."

Once more, Xstersi warmly embraced his son. "I've learned my lesson. Every Greeling counts!"

"He's right." Rumford's voice broke in over the speakers. "When I first laid eyes on the little, slime-ridden devils—it was the year Napoleon abdicated and fled France, my adopted homeland. Like him, I knew my dues had come home to roost! Punishment for callously discarding those I held most dear. So, they banished me to this infernal

Hell…" He broodingly worked the control-pad. "To perdition for us all! I'm sending the ship into the gas-giant below!"

"Won't he ever let up?" Xstersi muttered as they made for the exit.

-9-

They swam swiftly down the long, dark corridors. Xstersi and Yanxy each held Jeane in a tentacle between them to hurry their pace—going full out.

"Rumford, you don't have to do this. You can still redeem yourself. Come with us," Jeane beseeched him as they passed a speaker. Through a portal window, she saw the orange clouded gas-giant looming larger and larger. They wouldn't be able to escape the planet's gravity if they didn't reach their ferry-pod soon.

Still working the control-pad, Rumford shook his head. "It's too late for me, my dear. *Reichsgraf von Rumford*, Count of the Holy Roman and Greelon Empires, goes to his fate!" He pressed a final series of buttons. "You know, I presume, that liquid methane is highly flammable?"

The Autunite pulsed — and *all* the ionized gel-tubes running into it short-circuited. The kitchen burst into flame. It spread like wildfire in a chain-reaction down the corridor. Rumford prevented the emergency doors from closing. Liquid methane became a roaring inferno.

Jeane and the Greelons sensed the entire

ship tremble with the fury of the conflagration consuming it.

"We've made it!" Xstersi shouted as they swam into the ferry-pod. Looking out the cockpit, Jeane saw the gas-giant they orbited fill their entire view. They were falling into it.

"It's no good," Yanxy called out desperately as he worked the ship's controls. "Rumford's disabled the release mechanism. The water-lock won't close!"

Jeane glanced into the corridor. Across on the wall, she saw the manual override. But if she pulled it, how would she get back in? The water-lock would instantly seal.

The vessel shuddered. They were being torn apart. Jeane looked at Xstersi hovering near Yanxy in the cockpit. She saw how much he doted on his newly discovered son. What a shame to lose that now. Family bonds could be *so* fragile.

With a sigh, wondering why she was doing what she was about to do, Jeane swam out of the ferry-pod. At least someone should survive, she thought. Why not father and son?

Glancing over his shoulder, Xstersi saw her. "Jeane, what're you doing?"

She reached the manual release.

Turning at the sound of his father's voice, Yanxy quickly sized up the situation. "If you pull it, you'll never make it back in."

"I know." Jeane looked down the corridor. The searing glow of burning methane water reflected along the wall, approaching with blinding speed. There was no time left.

"Jeane!" Xstersi swam to the pod's exit. "Get back in here. I'll do it!" From within the ferry-pod, he reached out with one long, elastic tentacle, stretching it to the limit, across the corridor and around the release handle. "Hurry!"

Jeane swam back in.

Xstersi strained and ground his teeth. The flames came racing around the corner, straight at the open ferry-pod.

Xstersi pulled.

The door slammed shut, slicing his tentacle in half!

And they blasted away.

-10-

Gazing out the view screen as they shot to safety, Jeane watched the Imperial Flagship tumble into the planet's atmosphere. The ship appeared lit from within through hundreds of glimmering portholes as if by tiny, wavering candles.

Inside the hellish, blazing throne room, clutching the massive skeletal tentacles tightly around him, Count Rumford screeched, *"Vive l'Empereur!"*

Then the ship broke into a thousand shooting stars.

Jeane turned away. Behind her, Yanxy ministered to his father with the first-aid kit.

Xstersi winced as Yanxy wrapped a yellowish, seaweed-like substance around his severed tentacle. A troubled, but thoughtful expression overcame him. He looked uncertainly at Yanxy. "Tell me, what of my number — what of Wexter?"

"Dad! You never pay attention to anything going on in our family, do you? He's entered his hermaphroditic stage—and is laying his—*her* now —Quibble Eggs."

This last bit caught Jeane's attention. Quibble

Eggs came from—?

Yanxy continued. "I'm sorry I impersonated him, but it was the only way to get you to finance my expedition when I found those old transmissions in the Greelon Bureau of Records, pointing to the Emperor's lost ship. And... I suppose I also wanted your attention."

Xstersi patted his son's tentacle. "It's not your fault." Struggling to sit up, he turned to Jeane. "See what a lucky guy I am? Who would've thought it? From now on, I promise to keep my three brains more open-minded!"

Jeane concurred. "If you try to control everything, you're bound to lose out on any happy surprises—"

"Puh-lease, enough with your human moralizing, Jeane! Once a Greelon, always a Greelon. Am I right?"

Smiling broadly, Yanxy nodded in agreement.

Xstersi sank back onto the couch, exhausted from his exertions. He turned a pained eyestalk toward Jeane. "Oh, I nearly forgot. I have something for you." He grunted with a spasm of pain, unrolling one of his good tentacles.

He held up the very last Imperial Quibble Egg. "Sous-vide cooked just like you described. The advantage of many appendages!"

Jeane gulped. *Now* that she knew where Quibble Eggs came from... "Oh, that's alright. You should keep it."

"Yes, but I would like you to have it."

"It's not necessary."

"I insist."

"But it's the last one."

"Jeane, take it."

She hesitatingly accepted. "Thank you. I think I'll save it for—"

"Go on." Xstersi stared keenly at her.

With a sigh, Jeane rapidly undid her oxygen mask and popped the Quibble Egg into her mouth. She purged the mask of any water that had gotten inside, chewing thoughtfully.

"Well?"

Jeane swallowed hard. It was the worst thing she had ever tasted.

-fin-

RISING TERROR

Prominent inter-galactic Chef Hunter Jeane Oberon observed that an Earthling, Chef H.P. Lovecraft, once wrote: "conflict with Time seems to me the most potent and fruitful theme in all human expression." Oberon later amended the record, noting that Lovecraft wasn't really a chef. So, why did you waste our time, we asked? Oberon replied it related to the baking of a sourdough which nearly wiped out the Universe; the Galactic Culinary Society's chief librarian, Debii, was the only one to...

Excerpt from the Galactic Culinary Society's
Milky Way Review, Vol IV edition 3, N°317

-1-

Something's terribly wrong. I know it!

S Debii was having one of her frequent stomach-churning panic attacks. In the gloom of approaching night, her fears were always strongest. She had to double check everything before going to bed, so she went back to the library. As archivist for the Galactic Culinary Society, it was her duty to ensure that hundreds of delicate acquisitions were kept in perfect stasis.

She opened the door and flicked on a light, dispelling the shadows. Her tiny eyes glanced over the room.

She instantly knew one of her charges was out of place, but which?

And who had misplaced it?

Everything towered over her from her point of view. The library had been designed with an average-sized Sentient in mind. But Debii was the size and shape of a hairless squirrel. A *Hawaputian.* Only a small tuft of yellow hair grew behind constantly trembling ears. She wore white overalls, holding tiny arms close to her chest.

She nervously tapped her fingers.

The walls of the library were lined with illuminated cabinets kept at thirty-nine degrees Fahrenheit. Behind the glass fronts were shelves stacked with chilled Mason jars.

Hopping on a barstool, Debii peered in. "Rebola, Smedt, Vitus..." She ticked off the names of the starter yeasts, each from a far-off planet, each one-of-a-kind. "Mother... where's Mother?"

The glass jar which contained their most recent acquisition was open. And empty.

Something rattled behind her.

Debii turned and spotted a shadow slip up the stairs at the back of the library. She didn't have time to get a good look.

"Who's there? Come back here!"

Bounding up the stone circular steps, she was plunged into darkness. She cautiously slowed. *I should've turned on a light*, she realized. *But I need a stepladder to reach the switch and that would give the culprit time to get away.* She felt her way up the familiar stairwell, her nose twitching. What an acrid smell! Who could it be? Did the bakers who had delivered the sourdough starter have second thoughts? Had they come to reclaim it?

A pale glimmer ahead lighted her way. She emerged from the stairwell into a dark hallway where a shaft of moonlight fell on the floor from an arched window. She knew it looked into the courtyard of the old castle which comprised the GCS premises, but all she saw were the tall pines clustered around it, silhouetted against the night sky.

Debii hesitated. Her passion for her collection and impulse had brought her this far. But what if the thief intended to put up a fight? Maybe she should leave this to someone more capable? Of course, by then the trail would be cold.

She tiptoed warily down the hallway, thinking, *if I can at least see who it is...*

A distant heat-flash flared across the sky illuminating the window at the end of the hall.

Debii stopped in her tracks.

In the brief light, she saw a gray, bubbling mass like colorless slime stretch itself across the floor.

"Mother...?"

The clay-like *thing* disappeared around the corner.

Debii remained rooted to the spot, her mind filling with terrifying questions. It couldn't be? The starter yeast let itself out? But more, she'd sensed something... *horrifying.*

A cry came from the end of the hall. Jerked out of her stupor, Debii hurried on. Lord Hawktalon's tower room was around the corner. He was one of the *Overseers* of the Society.

A terrible stench assailed her as she fearfully approached the opened door to his room.

Lord Hawktalon lay sprawled on the floor next to his bed. There was no sign of the starter yeast. The white mask Hawktalon normally wore, hiding his features as per the custom of his race, lay to one side.

He looked up. What she saw chilled her to the bone.

Hawktalon reached out with one hand, imploring. His face was a rapidly disintegrating skull. "You're all going to die. I've seen it! Ol'Sands, Achiro… even Jeane… Oberon. Everyone!"

Then his body collapsed into dust.

-2-

Not far from the GCS castle, Jeane Oberon rappelled down a cliff-face under the starlight where black coniferous trees dotted the craggy mountaintop.

About a third of the way down, she stepped into the *Ansul* cliff-house cut into the rock face, releasing the karabiner attached to her belaying rope.

She stood in the entrance, inhaling the fresh night air, studying the dark valley below her feet. The sounds of night animals, a distant squawk, emanated from the trees.

Those old-time Ansul knew what it was all about, she thought, throwing her harness into the corner.

Whenever she visited the Society's HQ, the ancient castle-observatory on the mountaintop, she camped here. More cliff-houses were carved out of the precipice, but her explorations had proved this one to be in the best state of repair.

The Ansul, from whom they leased the castle—at a reduced price since it was also in a sad state—were a climbing species. Their modern cities were all concrete skyscrapers they crawled up and down like furry *Xenarthrans*.

Jeane grabbed a vacuum sealed nutri-bar from her cooler, unwrapped it, and threw it into the portable micro-box. Its glow lit up the cave-like surroundings.

In the morning, she thought, *I'll visit those two guest chefs, Bakers Wyr and Andë.*

The micro-box dinged and she munched on the flavorless nutri-bar, settling into her sleeping bag.

They came in on the same Transport Service vessel as me, she reflected. *Or were they already here? That's strange... why can't I remember?* She yawned, drifting off.

Through the cliff-house opening, an ominous heat-flash flared across the sky.

Or did they arrive after me? I should check the log on my wrist computer...

But then she was snoring.

-3-

"How could Mother have disappeared?" Baker Wyr loudly demanded.

He sat at a long steel table in the center of the kitchen next to his compatriot, Baker Andë. Both had camel-like faces, though Wyr was obviously older with long jowls and graying stubble. Andë was stout, broad, and energetic looking.

Debii sat on a stool guardedly watching the proceedings. In the morning, they had convened in the kitchen, a large, low vaulted chamber on the ground floor. An antiquated brick oven dominated one corner surrounded by dozens of modern devices of varying providence from across the galaxy.

"Forgive me if we're not too concerned with your bacterial yeast! Our Lord Hawktalon has disintegrated!"

This was the GCS's in-house chef, Tor-Brent. A gas-filled, balloon shaped creature from *Dobe*, he floated above the table waving his tendrils excitedly. Tor-Brent collected sight and smell from twin orifices above his oral cavity, so his species was especially well adapted for culinary work.

"Hawktalon isn't the only one to have disappeared," interposed Ol'Sands, another Overseer of the Society. "We found scraps of fur in Achiro's room. Whatever attacked Hawktalon, we assume the same thing happened to Achiro." Leaning on a walking stick, Ol'Sands was a bipedal, mole-like alien. Her eyes were clouded and blind. With Lord Hawktalon and Achiro Mifune apparently deceased, she was the remaining Overseer of the Society, the last of the *Triumvirate*.

As soon as Debii had raised the alarm the night before, they'd secured Hawktalon's room and searched the castle for *whatever* had assailed him. That led to the discovery of Achiro's remains. By then, it was morning; Ol'Sands ordered everyone to the kitchen to decide their next move.

"Maybe we'd better start at the *start*," Jeane Oberon suggested, leaning against a stone pillar. "I'm still having trouble following what happened. Debii?"

Debii felt much safer with the tall human around and was relieved when Jeane had finally shown up earlier; Jeane would know what to do.

"It's like I explained, Jeane, their starter yeast —which they nicknamed *Mother*—was crawling around."

"That's not possible," Baker Wyr retorted derisively. "We brought *Mother* here to entrust her to the Society. It's an ordinary sourdough starter culture."

Baker Andë shook his head. "I knew it was a mistake bringing her here."

"Well, I certainly couldn't have left her with you," Wyr answered back. "All you care for is what's *new*... everything has to be new! But what about our time-honored traditions? No, it was the right decision. If *Mother* isn't regularly divided and kneaded and fed with flour—from our original stocks—and water, she'll die! You'd forget to do it. You're too infatuated with anything that's shiny and new—"

"She can't die," Andë said. "She'd just go dormant—"

"Please," Ol'Sands interrupted them. "Two of our colleagues are dead!"

Jeane raised a hand for calm. "I know everyone's on edge, but I'm inclined to believe Debii. If she says she saw what she saw, then what they're saying might be relevant."

Debii nodded. Yes, Jeane would know what to do.

Jeane continued. "You're soon to retire, Mr. Wyr?"

The gray-stubbled baker nodded his overlarge head. "I can't go on forever. It's time for my apprentice, Andë, to take over."

"As if you'd ever trust me to run the bakery," Andë grumbled.

"Unfortunately, I don't have a choice. Only time will tell if *that* was the right decision."

Jeane ignored their squabbling. She had to keep

them on track. "How old is this starter dough you call Mother? From my understanding, starters can last for a very long time."

Debii wondered what Jeane was getting at? Did she already have an idea what had happened?

"I don't know. Millennia." The old baker replied. "It's true, a sourdough starter has its own heart, its own will. Mother is the *soul* of our bakery. But what you're suggesting… it's simply not possible."

"Jeane," Ol'Sands interrupted them. "Hawktalon and Achiro are dead. This is beyond your expertise. We're not police detectives. We need to get outside help."

"You're right, of course. But in the meantime, we're all in danger. With your approval, I suggest you call the authorities in Ansul City right away. Tor-Brent will watch over the bakers. They're not to leave this room. As for Mother, whatever *it* is… Debii, where are the flour stocks Wyr and Andë brought to replenish their starter culture?"

"I put them in the cellars."

"Then let's go see if *Mother* went to feed."

-4-

At the back of the kitchen, an antechamber led to a stone staircase descending to the cellars.

"Do you think the bakers know more than they're letting on?" Debii asked as they went down.

"They seem to be our prime suspects," Jeane agreed.

"And you believe their starter yeast has somehow… evolved?"

"I find it strange I can't recall how long Wyr and Andë have been here. Did they arrive after me? Or before? I've checked my wrist computer, but I can never remember the answer. Like it's in a fog."

"That's funny," murmured Debii. "Now that you mention it, I'm not sure either."

"It's as if they just showed up out of nowhere."

The stairwell opened into a dark, cluttered room. Boxes containing various artifacts belonging to the Culinary Society were stacked to the ceiling.

"You have your work cut out for you, Debii. Isn't this the fragment of coral recipe I brought back from Cor Caroli?" Jeane asked, glancing at an unopened crate.

"It's just me here," Debii sighed. "You know we're short-staffed. They barely pay me, but I like the work so it's OK."

"Maybe you need a volunteer?"

"Who wants to come all the way out here? And what about the yeast, Jeane? Aren't you afraid? Hawktalon said—"

"I remember."

They continued through the maze of crates. Debii trailed behind Jeane, watching from behind her legs.

The tiny librarian asked, "What do you think the connection is between the bakers and their starter yeast?"

Jeane was thoughtful. Finally, she said, "Every sourdough has a unique flavor. It comes from the lactobacilli in it: the bacteria. The yeast *is* a living thing, a fungus. When it metabolizes, the carbon dioxide it exudes causes the dough to expand and bubble, giving a loaf its holes."

"That's true. Even the microbes on a baker's hands influences the flavor of the bread," Debii concurred.

"Except—it's a two-way street. Just like the microbes from the baker affect the starter culture, over time, microorganisms from the yeast promulgate onto a baker's hands. You can almost say, a baker becomes their bread."

"If *Mother* is thousands of years old," Debii

reflected, "she would still contain the microbes of the person who first made her... *it*."

Jeane nodded. "Whoever created that yeast... is in some way still alive."

Debii shuddered at the thought.

"On Earth," Jeane went on, "Three preserved loaves, offerings, were found in a temple for the pharaoh *Mentuhotep*. They were four thousand years old. A physicist, Seamus Blackley, woke the sleeping spores and made a sourdough out of it. Time can play strange tricks."

"What happened then?"

Jeane shrugged. "Yeast dies when you bake it."

They stopped, arriving before a wooden door which was slightly ajar.

"That's the storage room," Debii whispered. "The flour stocks Wyr and Andë brought are in there."

-5-

A chilling presence radiated in waves from the storage room. The door was open a crack. Pitch blackness oozed out like from a yawning black hole.

"Jeane, shouldn't we arm ourselves?"

"Other than cutting implements, there's not much here. Besides, I don't think it would do any good."

They edged toward the door.

The blackness waited like a nightmare. Wisps of disorder and chaos tentatively reached outward, probing, searching.

Suddenly, Debii saw Lord Hawktalon's evaporating skull again. The terror of the night before washed vividly over her.

"Jeane, Hawktalon said you're going to die!"

Jeane looked grim. "I don't think our fate is predetermined." She stood braced before the door.

But it was too much for Debii. Everything swirled before her eyes.

"I'm sorry, Jeane. I can't!" She turned and fled.

Jeane faced the blackness alone while Debii raced through the maze of crates looming over her. It was like they were closing in, blocking her path.

Breathless, she sped up the stairs and into the light of the kitchen. She panted, sweat trickling down her spine. Then she felt ashamed for abandoning Jeane. *Why do I have to be so small?* she upbraided herself.

I should go back. But she couldn't get herself to do it, couldn't even face the dark staircase. Whatever was down there was too terrifying.

She tautly hopped on the table and glanced around.

Against the pounding of her heart, she saw she was alone. Where was Tor-Brent? Jeane had told him to watch over the bakers, who were also gone.

What happened?

"Hello?" Her voice was a tiny squeak. "Is anyone here? Tor-Brent?"

In response, she heard a faint noise like someone calling her name. It didn't sound like Jeane. Was it the GCS chef? Did he need help? Had the bakers attacked him? She turned around.

On the other side of the stair, under a stone lintel, the kitchen opened into the Lecture Hall. Had the sound come from in there?

Debii grabbed a frying pan.

She practically crawled on all fours past the steps leading to the cellar, willing herself forward, not daring to look down there. She crept into the adjoining room.

Something scuttled in front of her.

Scared out of her wits, Debii raised the frying pan and slammed it down.

Carefully, she moved it aside.

"Just a bug," she breathed in relief.

She looked closer. No! In embryonic form, tiny tendrils splayed around him, she recognized a vastly shrunken Tor-Brent.

She had just squashed him to death.

-6-

After the meeting, Ol'Sands left the kitchen and went up the stone steps past Tor-Brent's room and on to the third floor, pensively tapping her cane.

She entered the communications center. On the north side it opened into a hallway leading to her own quarters.

One stone wall was fitted with rusting and cobweb covered radio equipment linked to the astronomical gallery on the rooftop. Ages ago, it had been used by the quasi-religious-astronomical caste who'd built the castle, but it had long since fallen into disuse.

Ol'Sands shambled over to a worktable and sat down. The shoebox-sized, modern communications system lay next to the old array.

She switched it on but was surprised to hear only static. Fiddling with the touch-sensitive settings, she fine-tuned it. Still nothing. She made another adjustment.

"It won't work." Baker Wyr stood in the doorway. Ol'Sands turned her blind eyes toward him. "I disabled it."

Alert, but with an appearance of calm, Ol'Sands

reached for her cane next to the worktable. "Why would you do that?"

Wyr was strangely indifferent. "You're not like the others. You hide much... and know much. You're familiar with the *Uncertainty Principle*?"

Ol'Sands nodded. "We can never know both the position and speed of a particle at the same time." *What's the purpose of his question*, she wondered? Was he somehow trying to explain what was going on?

"Exactly." Wyr had a buck-toothed smile, but it wasn't friendly. "The closer you look at *anything*, the more it breaks down. If you could freeze Time —take a slice—at the smallest level, you would see the tiniest particle in existence. But you cannot stop Time. Not here. So, as you look closer, instead of a particle, you discern the Flow of Time, and *that* particle appears to stretch into a wavelength, like an exquisitely vibrating string."

"What do you want?" Ol'Sands demanded coldly. *Why these games?*

The baker ignored her. "Imagine you could live for billions of years—or were even *Eternal*—and had limitless size. You see a planet. There is an ocean. Waves. But what are these waves? For you, it would take a thousand years just to say *hello*. So, these waves seem to you like the smooth portion of a sphere... on a planet spinning so fast you can barely discern it."

"I take it you're not from around here."

"*When* we are from might be a better question.

But it doesn't matter. I won't let you stop *us*."

Abruptly, Ol'Sands felt something reach into her. "What are you doing?" she asked in an agonized whisper.

"You are getting older and younger. At the same time. I can't control it. With the others, it went very quick. You must be incredibly old."

Ol'Sands reeled as if her mind was being stretched across infinity. Her age was far greater than anyone in the Society suspected. Only this allowed her to hold on, just a little longer.

"What's happening..." Ol'Sands struggled to speak. "This *process*. If it goes unchecked... will spread. Engulf our universe."

"That is necessary for us to survive." Wyr watched curiously as Ol'Sands shriveled into a furless little baby, varicose-veined and wrinkled, incredibly old and young all at once. For an instant, the whiteness clouding her eyes faded and she saw with perfect clarity.

Then she vanished into oblivion.

Baker Wyr simply shrugged. "I don't really understand it myself."

-7-

I mustn't fight it, Jeane thought. *It's not evil.* She stood outside the storage room door. *I think it's... afraid.* She felt the strange waves emanating from it flow over her, threatening her consciousness.

I've got to keep calm. Try to communicate with it.

She approached the door, ajar, and edged in sideways. *Debii was probably right. This is a bad idea.*

A powerful sour-yeast smell assailed her which nearly made her retch. She took shallow breaths and waited for her eyes to adjust. A faint, grey light pulsed from the back of the room.

She saw the containers of flour stock Wyr and Andë had brought, black barrels, spread across the floor, split open. *Mother* lay atop the heap like a giant gray slug.

She'd grown to massive proportions: a humongous pile of colorless slime filling the room, pulsing, feeding on the last of the flour stocks.

Jeane took a tentative step toward it. Did the mass quiver in response? *Easy now,* Jeane thought.

Suddenly, an image flashed through her mind. Confusion filled her. *Nothing can escape. Blackness. Impossibility of light.*

Jeane struggled to control the feeling of overwhelming dread. She tried to understand the image put into her mind.

I was wrong! she thought. *It's not some evolved... It's not even a yeast, not really.*

She saw light — falling. Weighed down. Gravity, so great that even the fastest particles in the universe—light—were dragged back.

A swirling, red horizon. Within, the end of space and time. Was everything lost in that void? Could nothing escape?

Jeane recalled a theoretical class from her brief tenure in the Earth Guard: Thermal Radiation — emitted from a Black Hole. Information *can* escape.

But at random.

A Black Hole could emit *any* collection of particles.

Even...

I don't have much time, she realized. *I've made a fatal mistake. It's too late for me, but I can still send a message.* In her vision, she'd seen that only one of them was left.

She looked down at her wrist computer, but was transfixed by the sight of her hand fading, her atoms coming apart.

Quickly. Only a moment.

She tapped on the wrist computer, sending a short-wave signal. Would it reach—? No way to know.

Then her skin came apart like sand, the very

stardust of her being fell into the void, and Jeane Oberon was no more.

-8-

In a panic, Debii raced through the halls of the old castle, looking for someone, anyone. There was no one. What had happened? Even Ol'Sands' chambers were empty, filled with a desolate feeling like they'd been abandoned for centuries. Were they all dead? Was Jeane still in the cellars? Debii had an awful feeling something terrible had happened to her too.

What do I do? How do I get out of here?

She stopped and looked around. Without paying attention to where her tiny feet had taken her, she'd emerged onto the wall-walk under the open sky. It was grey and cloudy.

To her left rose the peaked, wooden roof enclosing the castle's immense, ancient telescope. A system of gears and pulleys opened it though it was rusted out.

Her gaze fell on Baker Andë sitting on the edge of the rampart.

"Don't go," he said.

She hesitated. Against an overpowering urge to run and hide, she felt something *else* compel her to stay. As her mind settled, as her breathing slowed, her curiosity crowded out her fears. She felt a strange desire to listen to him. *He wants to talk. Are his intentions benign? He looks so lonely.*

Andë nodded at the enclosed telescope. "Every intelligent species studies the stars. What they don't appreciate, is they're really studying Time."

Holding her breath, still fearful, Debii took a step closer and sat down.

"Before we bake our breads, we wait for the dough to rise. A precise time. *Everything* is about Time."

"I don't understand. What's been happening to us?" she asked.

Andë sighed. "Wyr is old and afraid. He can see the end. He thinks he can avoid it. I'm young. I have hope. But the end will still be the same. It is for you, anyhow—and now it is for us. But it wasn't like that *before*."

"Before what?"

"Let me try and explain. I've been doing a lot of thinking since we arrived. It's not easy for you to understand, I believe. Where to start? Yes, I know: how do you get from one planet to another—from one star to another?"

"There are *Wormhole Gates*. Built by a race that's vanished."

"Mmm, wormholes which cut through the folds and fabric of Space-and-Time as if it was a great, rippling carpet."

Debii shook her head. "I'm sorry, but I'm not a physicist. I don't know much about it." She wished Jeane were here. The human would know how to respond to this *creature.*

"Listen, anyone can understand. If an idea is true, anyone can understand. I sincerely believe that. Now, why must you travel this way?"

Debii was thoughtful. "Even when ships travel near the speed of light, it takes an incredibly long time to get between planets. And... the traveler on the ship ages more slowly. On returning, they'd be relatively young, I guess, while centuries would have passed on their homeworld. Without the Gates, we wouldn't have a functioning intergalactic community."

"Yes, very good! When two objects are stationary relative to each other, they experience the same passage of Time. But if one of them moves away—at a higher velocity—suddenly they experience *Time Dilation*. The slowing of Time is *only* experienced by the one moving at the higher velocity. Curious, no?"

"I—I've never thought about it like that."

"Why not? Do you realize that Space-and-Time are so interconnected that as you travel more rapidly, Space also changes? When you increase your speed, Time slows *even as* Space contracts and compresses like a finely kneaded sourdough. Unbelievable!"

"I suppose. But I don't—"

"Perhaps the Sentients who built the Gates understood. The races left behind know so little. Have you ever *seen* gravity? Do you know *what* holds the planets in orbit? How a pair of Quantum

Particles, light-years apart, can instantly know what their counter charge is doing? *Why* Time changes when you travel near the speed of light?"

Exasperated, Debii shook her head. Andë was so young and brimming with enthusiasm, she momentarily forgot the danger facing her.

Andë went on. "Do you believe in a divine being or that mystical forces control the Laws of the Universe?"

Debii shrugged. "My people have their beliefs, but I don't follow them."

"Then how can mass act on mass, when the thread which connects them, which you call gravity, is to your eyes and instruments invisible? There are two possibilities, aren't there? Either an all-powerful, magical being controls things, hidden, behind the scenes. Or else, there must be some mechanism, some *material* object which connects them?"

"Actually, though it's very expensive, we mine Graviton particles from the Wormhole Gates. That technology also comes from the vanished, ancient race. I'm not sure we understand it—"

"Excellent! Such a clever little thing! And what about Time? What about *it*? How can Time be relative? The people of your universe understand the math, but it might as well be a magical formula, for all it's worth."

Debii considered everything Andë had pointed out so far. She was stumped. "We don't know."

"Has it occurred to you that... there is no such

thing as Time?"

"How can that be?"

"If you consider it carefully, you will find there is only motion, only movement. Only the manner in which *matter* behaves… since *your* Big Bang.

"Out of that cataclysmic explosion, imagine an expanding field—forget about Time—of interlocked, infinitesimally small particles moving forever outward. Some of these particles become randomly twisted, forming the first subatomic particles. Then these also twist together forming atoms and so on. It's an expanding field of Space—*material*—and the way in which it interweaves, like a giant, stretching blanket, forms the laws of *your* universe. As particles amass into ever larger units, eventually planets and stars, these create depressions in the Field; the effects of gravity.

"And as an object travels faster and faster through this field—but never faster than the speed of light, since that is the rate of the expanding field—and remember, the *object* is also *part* of the field, just more jumbled together in units of what you label *matter*—compression occurs, mass increases, and so atoms spin more slowly—and *that* is why you age more slowly with increased velocity: the underlying processes have *slowed*, at least relative to the motion of other objects. It's all movement. Your universe is always in motion—moving outward—governed by the shaping of the Field of Matter at its inception."

While Andë talked, Debii had a vertigo-like sensation the stars were pin-wheeling above her head. When had night fallen?

She tried to process everything he'd revealed. What did it add up to? He was from *elsewhere*, trying to understand where he now found himself. How to respond?

"Thank you—for sharing—this—" Debii didn't know what to say.

Andë shook his head. His expression changed, and he looked at her piercingly. "What are you going to do about Jeane's message? Will you act on it?"

What was he talking about now?

"What message? I haven't received—"

"Never mind. Jeane is dead. *Mother* is on the move."

A chill ran through her.

"Your last Overseer is also gone. You're only safe because I've been trying to protect you. I want *someone* to understand... But there is a limit to what I can do." His eyes were like black pits staring into her.

She froze. Was he changing? What was this duality in him?

"You'd better go." He gave her a look, cold, like death and all the horror of the day before returned.

Debii fled.

-9-

Cowering, Debii hid under the blankets of her tiny bed, shaking like a leaf. She felt like she was in a nightmare. Paralyzed, stricken with fear.

When would the dream end?

How to escape?

It was as if time had ground to a standstill with no way out. Was it true what Andë had said? Was Jeane really dead? In her gut, she felt it to be so. She was the only one left.

Debii heard a strange noise through the chattering of her teeth. She held her breath, forcing herself to stop trembling. There it was again. A faint burst of static. Peering out from under her covers, Debii studied the room. On a wall-mount her computer flashed dimly.

Someone was calling. Who could it be?

She cautiously slipped out of bed and onto the stool by the computer.

"Debii, are you there?"

It was Jeane! Debii surged with relief.

"Debii, I'm sorry—I made a mistake—I don't have long—"

And just as quickly, she had a clammy feeling,

and all her hopes sank in her chest.

Jeane's message continued. "Debii—I've seen it —only you—Stop it. If you don't—entire universe —I know—You can do it. You're braver than—You have to—" The message abruptly ended.

Have to what? In distress, Debii yanked on the yellow tufts behind her ears.

She ran under the bed.

Jeane was dead. Andë was right. How had he known about the message?

She closed her eyes tight as if it could make everything go away.

Whatever Jeane wanted me to do, I can't do it! I don't even know what I'm supposed to do! The message was cut off. Who in their right mind would put their hopes in me?

For a while, Debii lay there not thinking.

Jeane said... I'm brave? Debii knew *that* wasn't true. *But Jeane believed it?*

She quietly thought. *If Jeane believed I could... Maybe?*

But what am I supposed to do? How to stop it?

Everyone who comes into contact with it...

And, it's getting bigger, spreading.

Debii recalled her conversation with Jeane when they were in the cellars talking about bread making.

A plan formed in her mind. She knew she didn't have long until the end of the universe.

-10-

Debii realized she couldn't get close to Mother, but someone would have to. At least, long enough to get the bait.

She faced the old stables in the courtyard. In a wooden stall stood a blue, rusting robot the GCS used for unloading cargo. In yellow letters across it was written: AUG-73.

Debii hopped on a barrel, reaching for a panel on the robot's side. She detached its controller and typed in a series of commands. The blocky robot lit up with a whir.

AUG-73 trundled out of the stall, making his way across the courtyard toward the kitchen and the stairs leading to the cellars.

I've got to observe him, thought Debii. *In case of a change of plan.* After all, AUG-73 was only a simple-minded robot.

Still, Debii couldn't bring herself to go down the stairs she had fled from in terror with Jeane.

Got to keep my distance, she reasoned. *If I end up like the others, everything will be lost. There has to be another way.*

She glanced around the courtyard at the

crumbling walls.

Yes!

She scurried to the north-western tower. Inside was an old, empty stone bath. She craned her neck, glancing up. Moonlight glimmered through the windows outlining stone grips inset along the interior wall. Ansul once used these to climb up and down between floors; stairs had only been added later.

With her flashlight, Debii traced the stone grips to the floor where an open space had been boarded over.

She tugged and heaved on a plank of wood, wriggling her way through the slim opening.

Sometimes it paid to be small!

She climbed stealthily down into the castle crypts. Her light fell on the granite tombs of former Ansul rulers.

Now, which way?

The flashlight beam played on the walls, the floor, catching a gleam.

It lingered for a moment on the long-forgotten bronze bust of GCS co-founder, Atticus Oberon, gathering dust, unceremoniously chucked in a corner when he'd been ousted from the Society.

She warily crept past the discarded bust, spotting piles of crates containing boxed-up GCS artifacts.

This time, instead of losing herself in the maze, she scrambled up the nearest stack, brushing her head against the ceiling.

She waved her flashlight.

It caught a blue-metal glint. AUG-73 emerged from the stairwell ambling toward the storage room, its door flung wide.

That's strange, she thought. *I don't feel... Mother's gone?*

Debii hopped from crate to crate, nearing the storage room's door. She carefully crawled down and peered in.

Oh, no, Mother's already eaten the reserve flour stocks!

Her flashlight wavered over the split open barrels while AUG-73 stood patiently in the center of the room waiting for instructions. *Mother* was nowhere to be seen.

What to do? Uncertain how to continue with her plan, Debii stepped inside.

It didn't occur to her to look up.

Mother clung to the ceiling, resting from her feeding, a dark gray mass blending into the stone.

Unaware of the danger directly overhead, Debii examined the storage area. Among the split open barrels of flour brought by Wyr and Andë, other containers and cans had been scattered about in *Mother's* frenzy. Whole storage racks had been knocked over.

Wait. What's that?

Debii's light caught something black wedged under a fallen rack.

Caught up in her search, she failed to notice the ceiling pulse with a faint glow.

There's one barrel left! I hope it's enough.

She tapped the controller and AUG-73 obediently trundled over, pushing the rack aside.

Above, *Mother* quivered.

Debii typed in a final set of instructions and hurried ahead, out of the room, while AUG-73 gently lifted the remaining barrel.

In her excitement, Debii scampered straight up the stairs she had been so afraid of before. AUG-73 mechanically followed, carrying the last of the flour stocks.

Mother detached from the ceiling and lowered her vast bulk to the floor. She slithered gooily after them.

-11-

In the kitchen, AUG-73 emptied the contents of the barrel into the large brick oven.

Debii took cover under the steel table where she had a good vantage point. Her heart was racing but she knew she had to stay and see it out.

Would her plan work? She'd find out soon enough. As Jeane had said, yeast dies when it's baked.

Something slammed onto the table. A shadow fell.

Debii watched the table overhead shudder as *Mother* rolled over it in a great, roiling mass.

She held her breath, her heart in her throat.

As *Mother* slowly moved across the table rust spots broke out in the steel like rapidly expanding sores.

Mother oozed off, puddle-like, and flowed over the robot and into the brick oven where the last of the flour stocks lay. AUG-73 trembled and shook. His blue-metal body turned brown, crumbling into a rusting pile of nuts and bolts.

Debii couldn't see that her own yellow tufts of hair had also turned white.

Now! She thought.

With every ounce of courage she could muster, she raced to the oven's 'on' switch.

She reached up and was bodily kicked aside.

She lay in the corner, panting, holding her bruised rib.

Baker Wyr looked viciously at her. "Don't you know I see what's coming?" he leered. He grabbed a meat cleaver. "It's you or us!"

He raised the cleaver. Debii closed her eyes, cowering. Then she defiantly thought, *I'm not going to go out like a coward.*

She glared fiercely up at him — and saw Baker Andë step behind, lifting a heavy iron pot. He walloped Wyr across the head. "You didn't see that coming, did you?" The old baker fell to the ground, senseless.

Andë's dark eyes turned to Debii. "You better go ahead while there's still time."

Debii shakily got up and limped over to the oven's switch. She hesitated. "What will happen to you?"

Andë shrugged. "Don't you understand? In this universe, everything moves *forward*. If a ball hits another ball straight on there's only one direction it can go. Forward. But we come from another place. Where if something strikes an object, it can go in any direction. Right, left, up, down. Try and imagine it. Laws of physicality completely different than your own.

"Mother, Wyr, and I are one and the same. I *am*

Wyr. He is me... when I will be older."

Debii glanced at the fallen form. How hadn't she noticed it before? But who'd have suspected? She saw it now, the resemblance. Only, his flesh was more tired, more worn down by the ravages of time.

"I'm still young with my whole future ahead of me," Andë said. "As soon as we came *here*, we saw. We saw how it would end. This moment. For us, inescapable. Where we were before, there was no past, no future. Only... *being*. Here, it's terrifying! How can life have existed before our own, while for us it was only a blank void, a nothing? How can we then have consciousness, so rich, so full of life—But then it too will be taken? This thing you call *death*. Oblivion. Wyr, being closer to our end, couldn't accept it. He thought he could change it—alter it. Unfortunately, in your universe, there is no escape from the relentless forward motion."

"I'm sorry. I wish there was something I could do."

"There is nothing to do but accept. And not waste any time. Just as there was my universe with its laws, and yours with its, maybe there is another. I can only hope. A place where my thoughts and actions will last. Where someone will peruse these frozen pages of Time. Even when I am long gone, I will still have existence when my thoughts reach out and touch *you*."

Debii looked sadly up at Andë.

"It's time," he said.

Debii nodded and turned on the oven.

Igniting, the gas-flame consumed *Mother*. Bit by bit, the castle filled with the warm smell of freshly baked bread.

-12-

Hopping on a barstool in the library, Debii peered in at her collection of sourdough starter-yeasts. She ticked off their names. "Rebola, Smedt, Vitus…"

Everything was in order.

She flicked off the lights, heading to bed, but had the unusual feeling of not being very tired.

Hadn't Jeane Oberon arrived recently, she thought? The human normally camped by the Ansul cliff-houses. Debii had a curious urge to visit them. Why hadn't she ever gone before, she wondered? For that matter, why did she always stay cooped up here in the GCS castle?

Feeling oddly brave, Debii was soon scampering under the dark trees, her way lighted by silver moonlight.

She hesitated at the edge of the precipice. The sounds of night animals, a distant squawk, emanated from the valley below. The sky was clear, and the stars were bright.

How beautiful, Debii beamed, inhaling the fresh night air. Below, she saw a faint light from one of the cliff-houses.

She swiftly climbed down and peered in.

Jeane was eating by the glow of a portable micro-box. When she saw the tiny librarian in the shadows, she warmly invited her in.

Moments later, both munching on flavorless nutri-bars, Debii listened attentively to Jeane's stories of traveling across the galaxy for the Galactic Culinary Society.

Strangely, memories of some other time and place kept flitting through her thoughts like pieces of a dream.

She'd have to remember to talk to Jeane about it later.

-fin-

Smoke Signals

-1-

I did it because I had to, Jeane thought as she lay dying. *Was there another choice?* In her gut, she felt she wasn't wrong.

She tried to move her leg where her ankle was broken. Pain coursed through her like lightning. She gritted her teeth, choking back a sob. Her whole body was on fire. *That* was the fever.

She clung to icy rock, looking up at the opening where she'd fallen through. Impossible. She could never climb out. Even with both legs. Nowhere to get a handhold. She had no strength left.

A faint ray of sunlight fell on her pained face.

Anguished, she looked down. A grotto domed with glittering ice; the walls were overgrown with black lichen. The air reeked of seaweed. At least it was warmer here under the ice.

Below the slippery shelf where she lay trapped was a wider outcropping of stone. A crackling fire burned there among the lichens she'd gathered, sending a thin trail of smoke skyward.

But who would see it?

I'm going to die on this planet.

She thought of *Achillion,* her mind churning with fever. She remembered.

Lying on the snow, leg broken. He looked at her through his white, featureless Skylar mask. Unlike other Skylar who kept their masks plain (and never showed their face), he'd painted two tribal stripes on his—fiery orange and red.

"We both know it to be true. If I didn't break you, you'd keep coming stubbornly after me. It's your own fault, Jeane! You started us down this path!" he shouted over the raging wind. So thick with snow she could barely see him.

"I guess you'll survive this storm," he rambled on. "Jeane Oberon always finds a way, isn't that so? And if you don't... It was a possibility according to the rules of our contest. If you hadn't cheated, I wouldn't have had to do this!" He turned away. She saw his back, his blue cape whipping in the gale. He disappeared into the snow.

Was he carrying *the Spear*? She tried to recall.

Yes, he had it.

Jeane closed her eyes. Fever, pain, and exhaustion swept over her.

Her nostrils tingled. She coughed. The smoke was getting thicker.

She opened a swollen eye and looked down.

Seawater rushed into the cavern between the spaces in the rocks. The tide. It was coming in. Faster than she expected. Her fire was quickly extinguished and sent up a last puff of smoke.

The ice-cold water flowed over her boots, then her thighs. Her legs felt an icy pang and went numb.

As the frigid seawater swirled around her neck, she vainly tried to stay above it.

Jeane wondered, *what's worse? Drowning or freezing to death?*

ABOUT THE AUTHOR

D. R. Schoel

Dana-Ryan Schoel is an award-winning writer and filmmaker who has worked for over twenty years with the Inuit of the Arctic on many television documentaries. He also collaborated with Chad McQueen (son of movie icon Steve McQueen) on an un-produced project for Netflix, and wrote the feature film "Adam's Wall", a Jewish-Arab love story, released globally. He directed the short film "The Fantastic Bus" which was presented at Cannes and, among other honors, won a Canadian Screen Award (the equivalent of the Canadian Oscars) for "Sol", about an Inuit circus performer who died in RCMP custody, which he co-wrote with Marie-Hélène Cousineau. In his spare time, he daydreams about following his cousin who's also from Montreal, William Shatner, into space...

BOOKS IN THIS SERIES

THE GALACTIC CULINARY SOCIETY

Curious to explore the galaxy? Brave enough to face many-tentacled aliens who'll disintegrate you on sight? If you're truly hungry for adventure, there's only… THE GALACTIC CULINARY SOCIETY! Let Jeane Oberon, Chef Hunter extraordinaire—if unfortunately human—be your guide to the dining rites of countless alien races: join the GCS today! And remember, it's an eat or be eaten universe out there!

The Galactic Culinary Society: Smoke Signals

A CONTEST LIKE NO OTHER!

Intergalactic Chef Hunter, Jeane Oberon, faces her most formidable challenge yet when a rival member of the Galactic Culinary Society lays down the gauntlet… to see who's the greatest Chef Hunter in the universe!

The race is on! Jeane travels to an icebound planet in search of a fabled spear known as 'The Eyes of Yvuru'. Only with it, and its power, can she track the legendary animal believed to inhabit the frozen world…

Journeying across a merciless landscape, Jeane's tested to her limits like never before. But far more than her reputation is at stake: Jeane's rival intends to honor the Galactic Culinary Society by feasting on their hunted prey—a creature on the verge of extinction, and the last of its kind.

Jeane will do anything to save it. Even if it means forfeiting her own life in the bargain!